I0580083

MARY CRAWFORD

Hearts OF Jade

HIDDEN HEARTS BOOK 3

COPYRIGHT

HIDDEN BEAUTY SERIES

Until the Stars Fall from the Sky
So the Heart Can Dance
Joy and Tiers
Love Naturally
Love Seasoned
Love Claimed
If You Knew Me (and other silent musings) (novella)
Jude's Song
The Price of Freedom (novella)
Paths Not Taken
Dreams Change (novella)
Heart Wish (100% charity release)
Tempting Fate
The Letter
The Power of Will

Hidden Hearts Series

Identity of the Heart
Sheltered Hearts
Hearts of Jade
Port in the Storm (novella)
Love is More Than Skin Deep
Tough
Rectify
Pieces (a crossover novel)
Hearts Set Free
Freedom (a crossover novel)
The Long Road to Love (novella)
Love and Injustice (Protection Unit)
Out of Thin Air (Protection Unit)
Soul Scars (Protection Unit)

OTHER WORKS:
The Power of Dictation
Vision of the Heart
#AmWriting: A Collection of Letters to Benefit The
Wayne Foundation

DEDICATION

This book is for everyone who
has felt like they no longer have the
strength to go on …
and yet somehow do.
You are a warrior.

If you find yourself in a position
where you think no one cares if you live or die
Somebody does. Someone *always* does.
Reach out to somebody, anybody — any way you can.
We are here and we care.

In memory of my friend, Valencia, who never knew
how many people loved her until it was far too late.

Chapter One

Jade

"Barbara Ann, why are you being such a drama queen about this? I thought we were getting matching Celtic friendship knots because I'm your best friend. Why did you let her choose the design first?"

The blonde sitting in my chair flips her hair back violently, almost screwing up my line. "Maybe you didn't get the first shot because you can't remember what to call me. The only person who still calls me Barbara Ann is my grandma — even *she* can remember to call me Lennox most of the time."

The girl who was whining looks really confused for a moment as she remarks, "Barbara — I mean Lennox — that doesn't make sense. It's not like we don't know your real name. We've been best friends since kindergarten. I don't get what's wrong with your name, but whatever."

The blonde in my chair huffs. "Ashley Nicole gets it. It bugs me that you don't. Maybe you aren't such a good friend, Allie."

Oh man! My head hurts too much to deal with this kind of drama today. I hated it in high school. I despise it even more now.

Allie rolls her eyes. "That's because Ashley Nicole likes to kiss your butt or make up some drama like she's gonna cut herself to get your attention. You play right into her game, too. You know she probably doesn't even cut herself, right? She just tells you she's gonna. Maybe I should threaten to kill myself. Would it score me bonus friendship points?" she suggests sarcastically.

"At least Ashley Nicole talks to me about more than how she's gonna pay for college. You're so boring that if you killed yourself, no one would miss you," the blonde smugly answers as if she's scored some sort of verbal blow.

The third girl, a tall willowy, blonde woman with round glasses who had been quietly sitting on the sidelines flipping through our portfolio books seems to realize a terrible line has been crossed. "Lennox, you shouldn't say stuff like that, it's not funny."

"Yes it is," she asserts with a loud snort of laughter. "Only losers commit suicide. If they want to leave the planet, why should I stop them?"

I lift my tattoo machine from her forearm and set it down on the table beside my chair. "You're done. Get out of my shop."

I walk over to my purse, pull out three one hundred dollar bills as I yank the stencil off the light-box and sign and date it. "This amount of money will get this design, three times over in any tattoo shop in this neighborhood. I'm not finishing your tattoo and I'm not asking any of my artists to work on you either. You might be pretty on the outside, but your soul is ugly."

The blonde looks at me with a blank expression on

her face. "What? What did I do? You don't like my name?"

Ashley Nicole rolls her eyes. "You moron, I'm embarrassed I ever thought you were my friend. She probably knew someone who committed suicide."

Lennox-What's-Her-Face snatches the sketch and the money out of my hand. She takes the stencil, crumples it and makes a big production of throwing it in the garbage. I shrug. I can't help it if she's a little dim. If she knew anything about me, she probably would've realized she could have gotten a few bucks for it on eBay. People are paying a crazy amount for even my signature these days since *Over It* became a huge hit. It's hard to say what she could have gotten for a signed and dated stencil. Unfortunately, you can't fix stupid.

She motions over her shoulder to her girlfriends. "You coming? Now, we can get ourselves some decent tattoos. I was afraid our tattoos would look like some kid drew them on, so this is sweet."

Allie and Ashley glance at each other in astonishment as Allie asks her friend, "Wait up! Do you know who Jade is? This is like, a once-in-a-lifetime opportunity? She's totally famous, they did a profile on her on *E!* You know, like on one of those be a celebrity for a day shows? She has some super famous clients — you know people on shows like the Oscars and the Emmys."

"I don't care who she is, she thinks she's too good for me. I'm outta here," the blonde chick waves dismissively.

Ashley Nicole gives me her best pleading puppy dog eyes. "If we're not like her, can we please stay? I would love to have a tattoo by you. I've watched your shows on

TV, and I love the charity work you do. I even helped out on a Habitat for Humanity house your partner did. I was part of a crew that helped out when I was in high school. I swear I'm not *like her.*"

Allie nods in agreement. "Yeah, I've always thought her Karma would bite her in the butt someday. She's kind of a witch."

I think about it for a few moments. "You guys are welcome to stay. I'm assuming you want to change your design. Given what you said, I doubt you want to pledge undying friendship to Ms. Barbara Ann."

Ashley Nicole shakes her head eagerly. "Hardly. In fact, I'll be finding a new ride to school on Monday. It'll probably be an interesting day, full of drama," she looks directly at Allie as she comments. "For the record, I don't do half the stuff she says I do, she makes it up so she can look all heroic."

Allie studies Ashley carefully. "For real? I'm not being played?"

Ashley Nicole holds out her pinky as she pledges, "I swear, I'm not kidding. She makes all this stuff up to make herself look like an indispensable friend. She's so popular around school, nobody questions what she does because if she's on your bad side, she can make your life hell. We're in college now and I honestly don't care if she is my friend. I'll catch a ride with somebody else. I don't have to put up with it anymore."

Allie nervously twirls her hair through her fingers and then seems to reach a decision. "I don't know if our schedules match, but I don't think I live very far from you if you want to catch a ride with me. I wouldn't mind the company; the commute is boring. Listening to the radio drives me nuts in the morning because they're always so freakishly cheerful."

The blonde girl pushes up her glasses on her nose. "As long as you don't mind stopping for coffee every morning, you've got a deal. I'll text you and we'll nail down the details."

I finish cleaning my tattoo equipment and dry off my hands. "Great, it sounds like we got everything all worked out. Now, does anybody have any idea what direction you want to take your tattoos?"

Allie slumps in her seat. "I have an idea about what I want, but it's not within my budget. Maybe I should wait. If I get a tattoo done, I want to make sure I get it done right. I don't want to look like Justin Bieber."

It's not often I have to do this, but I take back my initial assessment of Allie. Clearly, she's got more common sense than I initially thought. "I've got a little extra time because I'm not giving your friend her tattoo. Why don't you hit me with your idea and I'll see what I can do with it within your budget?"

Allie looks around the tattoo shop to see if there is anyone within earshot before she asks me quietly, "If I tell you my story, you won't tell anybody, right?"

"Of course not, everyone's tattoo story is very personal. I wouldn't be very good at my job if I started talking smack about people's private business based on what they told me. If you don't want me to share, I won't."

Allie relaxes a bit as she takes a deep breath. She starts to speak but then has to take another breath before she can begin. "I don't know why I always expect this to be easier every time I tell it."

Her words strike a chord deep within me. I don't even know what she's about to tell me, but I know that feeling oh so well. Every time I have to explain about Onyx, I feel the same exact way. Somehow, it doesn't matter that it's been eight of the longest years of my life. It seems like yesterday. Whenever someone brings him up, it's like I need stitches in my soul.

I hold my fingers up in the air in a T formation to indicate I need a break and then I go into the back room and get a couple of cans of pop. On impulse, I also grab a bottle of water and one of Marcus' ever-present energy drinks to be on the safe side.

When I return from the back room, I dump all the drinks onto the side counter where I usually have the portfolio books and announce, "I don't know about you guys, but whenever I talk about emotional stuff, I need to have caffeine and sugar to get me through. I didn't know what you guys liked, so I brought a little of everything."

Ashley turns to Allie, "I can leave if you need to talk to her privately. I totally understand."

"I'm sure you've heard all about it at school, or at least you probably thought you did. People never bothered to ask me what was true. Everyone assumed they knew what I was going through and, if they didn't know something, they just made it up and it became like a sporting activity to spread nasty rumors," Allie responds with a small shrug. "Finally, I stopped fighting."

Tears start to flow down Allie's face as she digs around in her oversized tote bag and hands me a notebook. The notebook is dog-eared and torn. There are dark, rust colored stains on it. While I'm carefully holding this fragile item, Allie reaches across my hands and opens it. I'm confronted with a drawing of a pencil erasing a terrorist holding an assault rifle. As far as political cartoons go, this one is poignantly beautiful. I don't know why she's showing it to me. My confusion must be clearly conveyed as I look to her for an explanation.

Allie looks haunted. "Callum drew it for me after the newspaper attack in Paris. Of course, I didn't know he would die in another terrorist attack — all he did was go to a concert."

My heart breaks for her. I have my own secret piece of art like this. A scrap of paper turned into a memorial I look at every time I take a shower. It's my own reminder of a life cut unbelievably short.

I can't stop myself, I reach out to hug Allie. "Memorial tattoos can be remarkably healing. I usually suggest inviting several members of the family. It's like a little celebration of life event. How does his family feel about this since they'll have to look at one of his drawings every time they see you?"

"I haven't spoken to them. Callum and I couldn't exactly be honest about our relationship because I didn't turn eighteen until October, and we had been seeing each other for several months before he died. If anyone had found out, he could have gotten in trouble, big trouble. I don't know if they even know I exist, let alone that Callum and I were planning to get married as soon as he finished his degree."

"Maybe you should tell them. Families are often desperate for tidbits about the last feelings and thoughts of their loved ones and that he stood up for something so worthwhile would make them so proud."

Allie wipes away a tear. "Yeah, being dead kinda

makes the three-year age difference seem like not such a big deal, doesn't it? What can they do? Punish him after he's dead?"

Allie reminds me so much of myself. I felt the same way about Onyx. I knew so much about him that no one else knew. After he died, I never knew which secrets I should keep and which ones were safe to tell. Nothing will happen to him now — even if the whole world knows every single secret. He was finally safe from pain and recrimination. "There's a certain logic to that," I acknowledge.

"I'm afraid. I haven't told anyone, no one knows — I mean officially. People talk crap, sure. Nobody knows the real story. Even my parents knew nothing about Callum. I don't think anybody from his family knows. He might have told his brother, Mark, but I don't know. Where do I even start telling people about our whole relationship history? People will think I'm making it all up or I lied to hurt people. That wasn't our story at all. We did it to protect our relationship. My oldest sister got pregnant when she was sixteen. I knew my parents wouldn't be okay with me dating an older guy. They would have never understood what I saw in Callum. Not to mention, he was everything my parents would absolutely hate on sight. He was an artist and a photojournalist. He loved taking incredible pictures and he even won some national awards for them — but drawing political cartoons was his passion. One day, he wanted to make the cover of the New York Times. I want to be able to tell his family all about the sides of him they didn't even know about."

Oh yes, I know all about the world of crushed dreams never realized because of a life cut too short. It is the saddest part for those of us left behind. We have to live with the knowledge of what should've been, could've been — what would have been possible if we could only go back and change that one split second in time.

Impulsively, I make Allie an offer. "Allie, you know at Ink'd Deep, we do memorial tattoos for free for service members and fallen police officers. Since your boyfriend was killed in a terrorist attack, I'd like to extend that offer to you. If you want, I can go with you to meet his family. I have had a bit of experience being the one left behind."

"Why?" Allie asks me bluntly.

"Doing memorial tattoos is our way to give back to the community, we've done this for a long time. It seems like the right thing to do."

"No, I understand. Why are you willing to do all the rest of it? You don't know me and the part of me you do know, you probably don't like because my friend was a jerk and I wasn't much better."

"The more I'm around you, the more I like you. We have a lot in common. I'm a little blunt and rough around the edges. Lord knows my friends should never be judged by the way I am around people; I'm practically like a wild animal. The social zookeepers let me out, but I have to be completely monitored at all times for fear I'll do something wildly inappropriate. My good friends are used to it by now, but newcomers are often a little stunned. Don't let that worry you though because I can be diplomatic and spot-on when it counts. I have my own reasons for wanting you to have the healthiest relationship possible with your boyfriend's family. If I can help with that, I'd be honored."

"I'd like that. Callum left behind other drawings and

I think his family should have them. I just don't know how to start the conversation. I'm sure they would love to have them. It makes me sad to keep them knowing they would cherish the memories if they only knew they existed."

"It might be best to wait a little while for your tattoo. But when I do it, that drawing will be phenomenal. I can't wait to get started on it."

I turn to Ashley Nicole. "What about you? Do you have an idea?"

Ashley blushes all the way to the roots of her hair. "I don't even know if this is a good idea. It seems like everyone else is getting this tattoo these days, and I don't want people to think I got it because it's trending on Twitter."

I shrug. "It's your body and your tattoo. If you like a design, own it and make it yours. Put your own little twist on it and ignore what everyone else thinks."

"You make it sound so easy, I wish I had your courage," Ashley flips through the portfolio again.

"Don't worry about it. It gets easier the older you get. It took me a while to grow a thicker skin. Look at me: tattoos and piercings everywhere. I get comments all the time. It seems everyone and their cousin's dog has an opinion about what I look like and what it means. They know nothing about me, but they seem to know all about my life based on a little piece of metal in my face. Piercing and tattoos are more popular now, but I've had these for years. When I first got them, they were considered odd and people reacted harshly. My advice is to get what you want because it doesn't matter what art I put on your body, somebody will disagree with your decision."

"I suppose you're right," Ashley agrees reluctantly.

"I did a huge back piece today and my shoulders are killing me. Why don't you and Allie come back on another day when my arms don't feel like spaghetti and she's got this whole thing sorted with Callum's family? Tell me about your design and I'll come up with some preliminary sketches for you."

"Great idea!" Allie nods vigorously. "We could treat ourselves to our tattoos as a reward for surviving our first set of finals in college. It'll be perfect."

"It will be if we survive." Ashley Nicole grimaces.

"I can't help but notice you still haven't told me your design," I gently tease. "Is it a naked guy or something?"

Ashley turns bright red as she laughs nervously, "No, it's not that complicated. It's a simple design, but it means a lot to me. It's a semicolon."

Before I can fully absorb the impact of her announcement, Allie gasps. "I forgot you knew Candace Jenkins."

"She was my next-door neighbor when I was a kid. They moved to another school district when her dad got a new job. We kind of lost track after that. I didn't mean to, but you know how it is. I heard she thought she didn't have any friends. If only I had known —" she breaks off with a small sob. "We planned to be in each other's weddings when we were little. We were like ebony and ivory — two sides of the coin. Now, she's gone for no real reason. I saw her parents at the memorial service. They were so sad, it was hard to watch. Her little sister — oh my Gosh! She may never be the same."

I have to wipe away a tear. "No, I can promise you she won't ever be the same. Her life is forever changed."

"Before Candace committed suicide, I have to be honest, I thought about it lots of times when my parents were getting a divorce. I thought maybe the world would be a better place if I wasn't here. After I saw what it did to Candy's family and friends, I decided I could never do that to the people I love."

"I wish my brother would have made the same decision," I confess.

Chapter Two

Declan

"What in the heck is she doing over there? She knows better than to start a tattoo and stop it in the middle. I thought she was ready to take over the business completely, but these days, I'm not so sure she's as dedicated to the business as she needs to be for me to be able to take a step back from Ink'd Deep," Jett works on my rib cage and observes the interaction from across the shop. "Maybe she doesn't have the sense to grasp it all, this is a man's world after all."

The man is holding a sharp implement to a very tender part of my anatomy, so I don't want to give away too much. He probably doesn't need to know I have more than a passing interest in Ink'd Deep's beautiful young owner. Maybe it's the long hair, my occupation or my current lack of permanent housing, but parental types like Jett are usually less than impressed by me. Street musicians are rarely who you wish for when you think of a potential son-in-law.

I stopped trying to justify who I am a long time ago. I go where I'm wanted. If I'm not wanted, I leave. It's seemingly simple. Honestly, it's a little more complicated than that. Some weeks I do well and can splurge a little and some weeks I eat a lot of rice and beans — or on some days, a whole lot of nothing. Lately though, I've been doing well. I have a circuit of places I've been playing that seem to like me a lot and tip well. It'll be interesting to see how that all changes after the beginning of the year when everyone's vacation is over, and life goes back to normal.

"For freak's sake, now she's crying over customers?" Jett mutters under his breath as he surreptitiously watches Jade. "What happened to my daughter who is hard as ice and never lets anything bother her? I taught her to be tougher than that. Where's her game face? Just a minute, Declan, I gotta go talk some sense into my daughter. For some reason, she's decided to be a girly-girl. She wasn't this emotional when she was five."

For some reason, I feel oddly protective of Jade. I've been hanging out at Ink'd Deep for a few years. I like the vibe here. They play lots of retro music and the artwork is phenomenal. Jett Petros gave me my first tattoo here a few years back, but frankly, I prefer Jade's style. She does amazing line work and shading. Her black and white tattoos have incredible depth. They look like they are able to leap right off of your skin. I watch as Jade takes a few swigs of an energy drink. "Looks like she's got it handled. If you talk to her now, you might embarrass her."

"You got that right, Ailín. She's as touchy as her mom when it comes to that crap. I don't dare say a word that makes Diamond look weak."

"I can see that. Your wife is one scary woman. I was at the library the other day, writing lyrics and I threw some paper away instead of recycling it and I thought Diamond was going to recycle *me*. If I hadn't been ready to go on the road for a gig, I think she was planning to make me check out books on recycling. She takes her duties as a librarian seriously."

"Don't count on being off of her radar quite yet, she's probably got you mentally tagged for community service for your infraction," he warns with a crooked grin. "She loves those kids in her reading program and she'll do anything for them."

Jett wipes off my tattoo. "Why don't you go check in the mirror?"

As I stand up, I remember why I absolutely hate rib tattoos. I walk over to the mirror and angle myself so I can see Jett's work; it's remarkable. You'd never guess I had freaky tribal stuff there before. He played off of the owl tattoo Jade gave me earlier and perfectly scattered feathers across my torso to cover my earlier work. The feathers look haphazard and random; it doesn't look like they are covering up anything at all. They are magnificent and the level of detail and craftsmanship is spectacular. "Oh wow! This is stellar. I've regretted this tattoo for nearly a decade and now it's gone. I can't thank you enough."

Jade wanders over to me and examines the tattoo. "Declan, you should've said something, I could have added these for you — unless you weren't happy with my work? By the way, great work, Dad. The placement of these feathers is a stroke of genius. It's a masterful cover job."

Faster than I can say a word, Jett is all over Jade. "I was under the mistaken belief you had three pieces scheduled for this afternoon. I see you couldn't close the sale on even one of those. What's going on? Don't you care about the future of the shop? We count on the revenue of the shop to pay the bills and the employees.

We have to have customers that book tattoos. This can't be a place where we gossip about makeup and hair. I taught you better than that, Girl. Where is your business sense?"

"I'd rather not sort out shop business here, but really, Dad? The Ink'd Deep I know cares more about the customers than the bottom line. We take the time to do proper consults, so we don't end up doing cover-up tattoos like you just had to do. We make sure our clients have the right tattoos for the right reasons. Isn't that what you always taught me? It's the whole reason behind the name: there's always a deeper meaning behind a tattoo. It's always about more than the ink. When did we forget that? The day we decide that's not important is the day I put down my gun and walk away. I don't care how much money I make at this; if it's only about the money, I don't want to do it anymore. In fact, some days I'm not sure I want to do it anyway."

"How can you say that? You've been tattooing almost as long as you've been able to walk. You have so much talent!" Jett argues emphatically. "Why are you suddenly doing stupid crap? Has the fame gone to your head? You don't stop a tattoo in the middle. You sure as heck don't pay a customer to go to our competitors. We can't afford to do that, and we can't afford to lose walk-in business. If you're gonna manage the business for me, you need to know this. What the in the heck were you thinking?"

"Daddy, I can't fight about this right now. I have an orchestra playing in my head. You can either trust my judgment on this one or not. Trust me, I had a good reason."

Jett walks over and grabs his daughter and pulls her

in close for a bear hug. "I'm sorry you're hurting, Baby. You know we have to talk about this someday… soon. The future of the business depends on it."

Jade visibly shrinks in her dad's arms when she hears those words. Her words are barely more than a whisper, "Yeah, Daddy, I know. Believe me, I know. It's not like I could ever forget."

I study Jade carefully and realize she is drinking another energy drink, but this is a different color than the one she was drinking before. "Hey, I'm about to grab something to eat. I absolutely hate eating by myself. People make all sorts of dramatic assumptions about my social life if I sit alone in the corner of a restaurant. Unfortunately, I haven't had a chance to visit your mom this week to see if she's got any new paperbacks for me. I would stick out like a sore thumb. Please rescue me and go to lunch with me."

Jade gives me a double take. "You go see my mom every week for books? Even I don't do that!"

I grin as I shrug. "Usually, I'm your mom's favorite customer. There was that time the Greyhound bus took off with my backpack on board and someone took off with my stuff. I wasn't your mom's favorite customer that week, but usually I am. I read so much she wants me to start writing a column for the library's website. I told her I'm not much of a writer. In typical Diamond fashion, she told me I was full of crap. She told me if I could write lyrics to a song and do poetry slams, I could write book reviews."

"What's stopping you?" Jade probes.

"I don't know. I guess I don't see how I'm qualified to write book reviews. I'm a musician. I write songs for a living and I play music to make people happy. I don't know anything about books other than what I like to read. Why should my opinion count?"

"My mom must have a good reason for trusting your recommendations." I help her put her jacket on. I notice she winces as she reaches back to put her arm in the sleeve. "Exactly how many books do you read in a week?"

"Usually three or four. If I'm going on a long road trip, sometimes it's more. Usually, I'll tell your mom in advance if I'm planning a gig a long way from home. Sometimes, she'll pull me a whole series of books. Your mom is a great librarian. She takes great care of me. Most people take one look at my appearance and decide I'm too dumb to read. I like to read even though I struggle with it."

Jade turns around and faces the back of the shop as she announces, "I'm not making any guarantees I'll be back today. I have a colossal headache and I don't have any more appointments booked today. My hands are feeling shaky from doing a huge back piece this morning, so the world might thank me if I stay away."

"Go. Go out for ice cream, go home, go out to a movie, or go do something crazy. You've been covering for everybody and no one's been covering for you. That's not the deal you made when you became a part owner. You're supposed to be taking some perks as part of the deal. I don't see you doing that," Marcus says from across the room.

"I went shopping with the spooky twins once," Jade asserts defensively.

"Ice, that was months ago," Marcus counters, using her nickname.

"It was not … oh I guess it was," she admits sheepishly.

I place my hand against the back of her shoulder as I gently lead her out of the store. "Come on, I know you have the heart of a warrior, but I am a mere mortal and I'm starving. If we hurry, we can beat Frannie's afternoon rush."

"Frannie's?" she repeats with a puzzled expression on her face. "What in the world is Frannie's?"

"Only the best eating establishment in all of creation," I answer. "Do you mean to tell me you are this close to greatness and you've never been there?"

"Yeah, I guess that's what I'm telling you." She rolls her shoulders and bites back a torrent of cuss words.

"Did you do that piece on Smoke's back all in one session?"

Jade shrugs. "Yeah, I know it wasn't my brightest move. I know better and I'll pay the price for the next day or two."

"Why did you do it then? You usually pace yourself better than that." I reach out and try to rub a knot out of her shoulder.

At first, she freezes at the contact. Jade and I have been casual friends for a while. Our social circles interact a lot and we have similar senses of humor. She's been supportive of my career such as it is. Whenever I post stuff on my Facebook or Twitter, she always shares that with all of her friends and she posts flyers in Ink'd Deep for me if I have a big gig coming up. I suspect if you asked Jade how I felt about her, she'd probably tell you I'm one of her buddies — if we drank more, we'd probably be considered beer buddies. The truth of the matter is, I'd like to be more than Jade's buddy. I've never figured out how to change who I am to her. I heard her tell one of her customers that no one respects her abilities as an artist because all they see are her boobs, lips and hair. I don't want to be "that guy".

It's true, I am deeply attracted to Jade — I won't deny it. There are many reasons I like her. She is an incredible artist and she is witty, smart and fiercely funny. Jade is a loyal friend and confidant. She is compassionate to clients and bends over backwards to make them happy. There is no getting around the fact that she is scorching hot. Her hair begs for a man to wrap himself up in it and get lost, her lips are the soft kissable kind and those eyes — those eyes will keep a million secrets and tell you everything you need to know.

Although we've been close acquaintances for years, this is the first time I've had the opportunity to give her a back rub. I wait quietly to see how she reacts. After a couple of seconds, she takes a deep breath and relaxes into my touch and lets her cheek loll against my forearm as she lets out a shuddering sigh and appreciates, "Oh man, that feels so good. I wish I didn't have to ask you to stop."

I shrug. "Jade, you don't have to ask me to stop. I'll do whatever you need me to do to take away your pain."

"Declan, you don't know what you're saying. My life is a bigger mess than you might imagine. There's a lot of random pain there."

"Isn't that true of us all? We're all a grand total of our life experience. Some of it's been great, and some of it sucks — what we put out into the world is a reflection of what has been given to us. How we process it determines whether we're winners or losers."

Jade chuckles softly. "I didn't realize you're such an armchair philosopher." As we stop in front of the restaurant and I open the door, she twists her back to loosen it. "Trust me Declan, you don't want me to dump on you. Some days I feel like I have the weight of the world on my shoulders. It wouldn't be fair to you."

I flex my muscles a little. "I don't know, I think I can probably handle it. I've got broad shoulders."

Jade scoffs. "Oh, I wouldn't argue that you don't have nice shoulders, it's too bad you let some poser scribble all over them. Lucky for you, I fixed your mess. I hope you learned your lesson about letting a semi-drunk friend practice his tattooing skills on you."

"Hey, I thought I was being a good friend," I argue in my defense. "He didn't tell me he was drunk until he was halfway through the tattoo. By then, I was already committed and there wasn't much else I could do. Besides, it will never happen again. I swear I'll never get any artwork done outside of Ink'd Deep."

Jade grins at me and her whole face lights up. "Never let it be said that I don't like a smart man." She's beautiful on any day, but when she's being mischievous, it's a whole other kind of gorgeous. She picks up the menu and studies it. "What's good here?"

"Everything!" I sigh contentedly as I rub my belly.

Jade shakes her head abruptly. "No, I mean it. What's really good? Don't take the coward's way out, I know every restaurant I've ever been to has its own specialties and the rest of the stuff they do is mediocre."

I set my menu to the side. "Okay, I hear you now. Personally, I dream about her meatloaf sandwich when I'm on the road. It's that good. I also crave the open-faced roast beef and gravy sandwich and the turkey dinner. This is one of the few places you can get a turkey dinner year-round. I love being able to get turkey and stuffing with cranberry sauce in the middle of summer."

Jade holds her hands up in surrender. "I give up. I'm starving and I have to resort to inviting myself over to Rogue and Ivy's mom's house if I want some decent home cooking. Mama Rosa and Isaac have started calling me their ghost daughter because I'm over there so often. I'd love to have some roast beef and gravy. My grandpop used to have it all the time. He swore if he ate it before baseball games, his team never lost. Even when I was nine, I knew that wasn't exactly true, but I never pointed it out to him. I liked our mealtime ritual before games."

"That's a sweet memory. In my family it was corned beef and cabbage. They would always make a big pot of it before church and then everybody would eat before watching the football games on Sunday. Well, the family members that didn't have to work. Most of my family works at the lots on Sunday, so it's not like we have a huge gathering or anything. There's something that's so great about corned beef and cabbage. It can sit around for a few hours without much damage. People could come and graze on it as they needed to."

"Lots? What do you mean lots?" Jade asks with a befuddled expression.

"Ever heard of Stone Auto? 'Our cars are as solid as granite, but our prices are rock-bottom'. That's my family. It's been in the family for generations and there will likely be many more. I was one of the few to escape — much to my dad's chagrin."

"Of course I've heard of them. Everybody in Florida has heard of them. It's a gargantuan company and they have ads everywhere. Do they still give a pet rock out to every kid who gets dragged along when their parents buy a car? I always thought that was kinda cool. I'm confused though — your last name isn't Stone."

"It is, and it isn't," I reply. "My family is an interesting mix of very prideful people. When my grandfather emigrated here from Greece, he decided Ailín didn't sound American enough, so he changed it to Stone to fit in. The names mean the same thing."

"Wow, isn't that funny? Our last names mean the same thing, but Declan isn't Greek, is it? It sounds Irish," Jade comments.

"That would be my mom's side of the family who wanted very much to keep naming traditions alive in the family. Apparently, I am named after a great uncle."

"You have met most of my eccentric family, Jade, Jett, Diamond … and Onyx. I'm sorry you didn't get a chance to meet my brother, but are you sensing a pattern here?"

"I like your name I think it suits you well. It's beautiful like you," I compliment like the gentleman my mom taught to me to be.

Jade groans. "When did you turn into such a cheese ball? I think I liked you better as the armchair philosopher."

"Hey, I might resemble that remark. I write lyrics for a living. I thought women liked this sappy stuff."

"I don't know, maybe some women do. You should know by now I'm not like most women. Maybe I march to a different drummer or something, but it sounded like a lame line to me. It sounded like something you'd say to any old woman in a bar or at a club to pick her up… it's skeevy."

"Wow! Talk about your fundamental misunderstanding. I was trying to be nice. I do happen to think you're very pretty and that your name reflects your personality and your beauty very well. I wasn't trying to be creepy at all," I explain in an attempt to clarify my remarks. "If that's the way I'm coming off, perhaps I need to work on my interpersonal skills."

Jade takes a long drink of her iced tea and then sets it down on the table. She runs her fingers through her hair and then takes a rubber band off her wrist and puts her hair in a ponytail. I try not to cringe because I like her hair down and wild. Having long hair myself, I know why she puts it back. It can be a pain to have it fall in your face all the time. When she finishes fiddling with her hair, she sighs. "Look, I'm sorry; I might be a little oversensitive. It's been a crazy long week."

"Is there anything I can do to help?"

"Sadly, I don't think so. Unless you can change a lifetime of expectations. It's complicated and I don't think there are any great answers. If there are, I haven't come up with any and I've been trying to work it out for months, if not years."

"I know that feeling. Sometimes you have to do what's right for you — even if it hurts the people you love."

"Really? Because you know all the people I love. Do you think I'm big on hurting them?"

"I know you're not. It's all a difficult balancing act. But, sometimes you have to watch out for yourself, too. What's your dilemma?"

"Declan, I don't know if I should tell you. First of

all, you'll think I'm crazy and secondly, you're technically my dad's client," she argues after the waitress puts our food down in front of us.

I silently ponder her arguments as we eat our lunch. After a few bites, I respond, "I usually try my best to see both sides of an issue before I make up my mind. I'm as much your client as I am your dad's. Besides, where is it written that you have to have some sort of sacred relationship with me like a priest or a doctor? We're friends."

Jade takes a deep breath and blows it out. "Okay, it's not like I have anybody else to tell this to. Marcus is too busy making googly eyes with his wife. Ivy's friend Jessica is cool, but she's got Mitch now. I can't tell my own family because they're part of the issue."

"If there's anything I can relate to, it's family being the issue," I commiserate.

"So, what you're telling me is if I completely unload on you, you won't go running to my parents to tell them what I said?"

"I told you I had broad shoulders and I meant it. If you need to talk, I'm here for you."

"I hope I don't regret this decision." Jade pushes her plate away. "Do you ever wonder if you are destined to do something with your life that's completely different from what you're doing right now? I mean, the entire world thinks I'm wickedly talented at being a tattoo artist. I suppose I probably am, but I don't know anything else. I've done this since before I could write my name. You know my dad had me practicing on old ham hocks when I was in preschool? I know how to shade and layer designs instinctively. I'm grateful to my parents for that knowledge. I can never thank my parents enough for what they've taught me. I know so much about art because of what my dad taught me and so much about literature and books from my mom."

"Your parents are great, so what's the problem?"

"My parents want to retire and travel. My dad wanted my brother to take over the business, but now that's not possible, so it's all on my shoulders."

"Maybe you could talk to your brother and ask him to share more of the burden."

Jade looks stricken for a moment before tears gather in her eyes. "I wish I could, but I can't. I forgot you were touring in Mexico when it happened, so you probably don't know. My brother committed suicide during his third week of his freshman year of college. My parents never talk about him."

"I swear I don't *try* to be a jerk, When I came back into town everything with the shop had changed and I thought something must've gone wrong with the remodeling project or something — they had your street shut down for weeks and I figured business was slow. I didn't ask any questions because I didn't want to stress anybody out. I'm so sorry Jade, that must've been awful."

"It's the worst pain I've ever been through in my life. Even though he was older than me, we were sort of like twins. We lived out of each other's pockets. People said we were like two sides of a coin. I don't know if I'll ever be whole again. It's like part of my heart is missing — the syncopation is off in my life."

"I can only imagine. But how would stepping away from Ink'd Deep help? That place is as close to a family as I've ever seen, even if you take your dad out of the equation."

"Onyx was supposed to be my path out of the business. We had it all planned out. He knew what I wanted to do, and he was totally supportive. He would go to college to show my dad it was safe for me to go away to school. The plan was Onyx would major in art so he could come back and work at the tattoo shop. He was the one who was supposed to take over for Dad. After he finished school, I could go to college and become a teacher. I wanted to teach kids about the power of learning about arts and English and being creative. More importantly, I wanted to teach about being true to yourself, sticking up for who you are, and the power of believing in yourself and your dreams."

"That sounds like an amazing plan, I'm sorry it never had a chance to come true. The world needs more teachers with your kind of passion."

"You have no idea. Onyx, my beautiful, talented, creative brother, killed himself because some strange kids he barely even knew convinced him he wasn't worth anything because he was different from them. What if more people had been in his life to teach him to stand strong and believe in himself when others didn't? Would he still be here today? What if my role in life isn't to draw pretty pictures on people's bodies, but to be the one voice in someone's head that reminds them they are worth it when they feel like they are out of choices?"

"Don't take this the wrong way, Jade, but do you know teachers make crap pay? Although I don't know exactly how much you make at Ink'd Deep, I know it's a solidly successful shop and your pieces go for a premium amount of bank. You are more booked up than any other tattoo artist in the shop; believe me I know. I've tried to make an appointment with you — I know personally how hard it is."

"Yeah, so?" Jade snaps at me.

"You have an incredible, God-given talent as an artist, and it would be a shame to lock that away in the classroom somewhere so they could pay you pennies. You could be making tons of money that you could give to some charity somewhere where they could put qualified professionals in the classroom to help teach those skills you want students to have."

"Hey, Declan? Does your family think you're good at the art of the sale?" Jade asks me in the ultimate non sequitur.

"Yeah, they call me a natural, why?" I'm puzzled by the change in the topic.

She throws her napkin on the table. "Finish your lunch, Declan. Suddenly, I'm not hungry anymore. I'm going home."

CHAPTER THREE

JADE

As I dip my big toe into the bathtub to assess the temperature, I start to mentally tear myself apart. I wish Onyx were here. He would've been able to instinctively tell me whether I should have trusted Declan.

I don't know what I was thinking. I know better. Maybe I was taken in by his beautiful face, his chiseled jaw, that gorgeous hair, or his impossibly long eyelashes. Beats me. I know I shouldn't have trusted him with my memories of Onyx or my hopes and dreams. He's no different from everyone else I know. Declan must think I am nothing more than some weird child prodigy.

It all boils down to dollars and cents. Nobody understands I've never had a chance to explore anything else or decide what my career should be. Maybe I never wanted to be an artist or maybe I'm not the wild, crazy celebrity-chasing, social media icon people want me to be. Once upon a time, someone decided I'm an iconic social media character. It's ridiculous because the whole image was invented. The Jade they think exists is largely a figment of their imagination. She has very little in common with the person I truly am. They've pegged her as being outrageous, plastic, flamboyant, sassy and mean.

I'm not any of those things.

My idea of a fancy evening is whipping out the genuine Dutch chocolate my parents bought on their last European vacation and sitting in front of the fireplace reading a great bestseller. I have a Kindle and read books on it all the time. Occasionally, I'll splurge and buy a signed paperback edition. It's sort of my weird, odd collection which no one understands. I guess you have to be a true bookworm to understand my love affair with signed paperbacks. If I love the book, I'll go to great lengths to find it in hardcover. I know it's a rarity when my parents buy both a signed edition and good chocolate. I study the gift basket. Maybe my dad feels guilty for all the extra pressure he's been heaping on me.

I figured maybe talking things out with someone else would help me make sense of all the thoughts rolling around in my head. Unfortunately, I think it made it worse. I guess I thought Declan might have my back a little more solidly. I figured as an artist, he would understand my need to be true to myself. Honestly, I thought he would be a lot more like Onyx and a lot less like my dad or the creepy career counselor in high school who kept trying to convince me I should join the veterinary sciences class because animal husbandry is a lost art and there's a lot of money in it. That may have been true, but there was one problem: I'm deathly afraid of large animals. Mitch's search and rescue dog, Hope, is pushing every boundary of comfort I've got — although I have to admit she's growing on me.

Of all the people I thought might be judgmental of my potential choices, Declan wasn't one of them. The man is the definition of a free spirit. He carries virtually everything he owns on his back. As far as I know, he doesn't even have a home. He is one of many people in town who use Ink'd Deep as their personal mailbox. When Marcus married Ivy, he built a set of wooden lockers and messaging system with Isaac, his new father-in-law, for ex-employees and long-term clients like Declan. If our space had showers, I think Declan would live at Ink'd Deep. He's always been supportive of the tattoo shop, but I expected him to be more supportive of me. I would've never pegged him for a guy who would support traditional values. As far as I know, he bucks any and all traditions on principle. Why is it okay for him to go against everything conventional, but want me to follow tradition to the letter? That doesn't seem right.

Usually, Declan is all about the fairness in life. I've seen him take money out of his own pocket to buy a toy for a kid if he sees the parents showing blatant favoritism between their children just so he could level the playing field.

I wish Onyx were here to talk to. He understood me better than anyone. He would know what to do in this situation. He would probably have some pithy advice that was equal parts painful and funny, but yet so spot on I could never afford to blow off his advice even if I was tempted to be offended by it. I thought he shared everything with me too, but I guess I was wrong. He didn't clue me in until it was way too late. I almost made it in time, but not quite.

I'll never forget that day for as long as I live. I decided I was too impatient to wait for the master plan to come together, so I took online classes at the local community college. I had to attend an in-person orientation session to get started. As I was waiting for my class to begin, I got what I later learned was a goodbye letter from Onyx.

I didn't know what it meant at the time. The tone of the letter was strange, and it was something my brother would never write if he were in his right mind.

I had visions of somebody holding a knife to my brother's head and making him write something under duress. I had no idea what was wrong. I just knew I had to get to him and figure out what was going on, so I left a note for the professor and left it on the top of the lectern. I ran out of the class, practically mowing the professor over as I mumbled something incoherent about a family emergency.

I threw my book bag into my car and drove nine hours straight to get to his school. I stopped only to go to the restroom. I'm not even sure what possessed me. I guess instinctually I knew on a soul level something was terribly wrong. When I finally reached his university, I made up a story to tell his RA about my brother needing medication. The RA finally relented and let me into Onyx's room. What we saw when he opened the door will haunt our dreams until the day we die. We both stood in stunned silence as we tried to make sense of what was in front of us. I can make guesses, but even all these years later, I don't know what could've possibly been so wrong in my brother's world to make him hang himself from the ceiling rafters in his dorm room. My brother, who lived to make people laugh and inspire the world with his art, died in the center of the room with a belt and a chair while he wore a pair of old Levi jeans with a hole in the knees. My brother was always a compulsive neat freak. The only other thing in his whole room which looked remotely out of place was a single piece of paper written in his scraggly print which read, "I'm sorry, I couldn't handle the hurt anymore. Even hell has to be better. Mom and Dad, I love you. Jade, go conquer the world — you are stronger than me."

I rinse the washcloth off with ice-cold water and ring it out again as I place it over my eyes. Hot tears are streaming down my face as I remember my brother. Onyx had it wrong. I'm not strong; I'm not strong at all. I'm a complete mess. Some days I miss Onyx so much, I can barely breathe. Everybody expects so much of me and I'm afraid someday I'll crack open and show the world there's nothing inside of me, and I'm a fraud.

I take a deep drink of my hot chocolate and rest my head against the back of the tub as I sink into the warm water and try to rest more. This headache is beyond ridiculous. I've tried everything I can think of from over-the-counter stuff to searching Facebook for popular remedies. It seems like I'm getting more intense headaches these days. It's no wonder though, it seems like I have responsibilities coming from every angle. I can't catch a break. If I could solve one area of my life, it might be a little easier. Every time I try to resolve one area of my life then something else blows up. I feel like I'm playing some twisted game of Minesweeper.

My phone starts to ring and it's not a ring tone for one of my friends or my parents, so I dry my hand on the towel I left on the edge of the tub and answer the phone, "Hello?"

"Is this Jade Peters?" an unfamiliar voice on the other end of the phone asks.

"I'm Jade Petros, is that what you mean?" I answer, confused by the odd question.

"Oh, so it is. I can't even read my own chicken scratch," she replies with a self-deprecating laugh.

"I'm sorry to be rude, but who are you and why are

you calling?"

"That's right, I didn't introduce myself. I'm one of the patient coordinators at Shands. We found your friend lying unconscious today. He had nothing on him except this card with your name on it. Apparently, he is urgently asking for you. We don't have any other information on him. He doesn't have a wallet, a cell phone or anything else. He keeps calling out your name. Would it be possible for you to come down and see him?"

"Who is it? Is it my father?" I inquire, my heart beating a million miles an hour. Marcus has done a great job of making sure Ink'd Deep is as secure as it possibly can be, especially since Rogue married Tristan, a security expert. Still, some of our clients have interesting pasts, so to speak. Some histories are darker than others.

"No, I don't think so," she replies. "Not unless your dad is a young man. This gentleman keeps saying his name is Pelican. At least that's what we think he's saying, it's hard to say with all the swelling around his mouth. He's in rough shape, but he wants to talk to you. We don't have any other contacts for him except you; is it possible you could come see this young man?"

"Is it Declan?" I ask, my voice raising in alarm. "Does he look like he belongs in a rock band somewhere?"

The woman chuckles. "Yes, I suppose he does fit in to the MTV generation."

"Listen to me! You have to tell the doctors not to give him any morphine. He told me once that it would kill him."

"Oh goodness! Just a moment —"

I peek around the curtain as my heart beats in my throat. The last time I was anywhere near a hospital, we were afraid my dad was having some sort of major heart incident. It turned out he had developed an ulcer after my brother died and he mistook the symptoms for a heart attack because Grandpa died that way after one last stroke. It was scary either way.

When I see Declan, it's all I can do to not cry. If it were not for his trademark long hair, I wouldn't even know it was him. He is virtually unrecognizable. Thank goodness he's sleeping, because I can't pretend to disguise my reaction to his appearance. I'm not much of an actress. That would be Jessica's area of expertise, as a Theater Arts major, not mine. False fronts aren't my thing. As I walk around the bed to the chair sitting beside his bed, I notice his hand is all bandaged. I can't catch the gasp of surprise that flies out of my mouth.

Unfortunately, this causes him to open his eyes. "Hi Ja —" he whispers weakly.

I sit quietly in the chair beside his bed and fiddle with his sheets to straighten out any wrinkles as I say, "Hi, yourself. Apparently, I can't leave you unsupervised for any amount of time. I only left you a little over six hours ago. What did you do to yourself?"

Declan tries to focus his eyes on me but his left eye is swollen so much he can't even open it. It looks like a big purple eggplant. His beautiful strong nose is definitely broken and there are stitches across the bridge of his nose. I wonder if it will heal with a bump like Onyx had after he hit his head on the neighbor's diving board in the eighth grade. Declan starts to cough and wince when he tries to talk.

I lay my hand on his forearm. "You know what? Never mind. The details aren't important right now. We can sort all this out later. You get some sleep, I'll be right here in case you need anything."

Declan gives me a thumbs-up with his good hand.

I study him briefly. "Do you want me to clean you up a little? I promise to be gentle. I used to give my grandma sponge baths all the time before she passed away. All the gunk on your skin can make you itch."

Declan gives me another thumbs-up as tears leak from the corner of his eyes.

I've tattooed this man for hours on end with intense line-work and shading. I have never seen him show any sign of pain. Alarmed, I ask, "Should I get a nurse? Do you need some pain medicine?"

Declan shakes his head as a tear slides down his face. He tries to wipe it off with his bandaged hand and gives a growl of frustration.

I grab some Kleenex from the bedside table and wipe the tears from his face.

"Relax, Dec, I got this," I assure him. I walk over to the sink in the corner of his room and pour some warm water in a little dishpan I see sitting there. I wish I had my soothing facial wash, but all I have is the pink hospital soap. I guess it will have to do; I squirt some on a washcloth and leave one washcloth without any. I walk back over to the side of his bed and pick up his uninjured arm. "If this hurts, let me know."

As I begin methodically cleaning off his body one inch at a time, the full extent of whatever happened to him becomes clear. Very little of Declan Ailín remains untouched by whatever calamity overtook him. The man even has bruises behind his kneecaps. Why in the world would he be injured behind his kneecaps? The other thing I can't help but notice is how utterly beautiful this man is. I guess I've always known, but I haven't been this up close and personal with him before to appreciate the perfection in his physical form.

When I make my way up to his hair, I notice it's matted with blood; there isn't a lot I can do about it under these circumstances. I look around the room for things to clean and tame his wild mane of hair. Unfortunately, there's not a lot in the cramped, sterile room. Suddenly, I remember Marcus gave me a gag gift to go with an 80s costume we wore to a fundraising dinner for Habitat for Humanity a couple of months ago. It's probably still at the bottom of my big, oversized purse. I put the dishpan back over by the sink and dig through my purse. It's all I can do to not break out in a victory dance when I find the garishly colored vintage comb with widely spaced teeth and a large handle in the bottom of my purse. Although it's not very helpful for my half African-American/half Greek hair, it will work beautifully on Declan's long locks.

I go back over to the sink and run a new dishpan full of warm water and grab a clean washcloth. With painstaking care, I use the washcloth to remove large clumps of blood as I comb gently through his hair. At first, I was worried about causing Declan more pain. However, he seems to have drifted off into a somewhat peaceful sleep. I wonder if they gave him some pain medication because he doesn't even seem to notice when I accidentally pull his hair when I encounter a stubborn tangle. Finally, after almost forty-five minutes, I have completely combed through as much of his hair as I can reach without disturbing him. I fanned it out around his head like some oddly imperfect halo.

As I sit back to evaluate the status of things, I notice his lips look dry. Sleep is probably more important right now than getting him something to drink. I fish out one of my many tubes of Chapstick from my purse and take the seal off. I guess Declan is lucky I can't seem to pass a checkout stand without seeing if they have any unusual flavors of Chapstick. This particular one happens to be pineapple. I hope he likes it.

I'm concentrating as I slide it over his lips to make sure I don't hit any obviously injured spots too hard, so I'm startled when his hand reaches up and grabs my wrist in a surprisingly strong grip as he harshly whispers, "Dammit, Jade, I've always wanted you to touch me, but not this way."

CHAPTER FOUR

DECLAN

WHAT IN THE HECK happened to me? I haven't hurt this bad since my cousin tried to fix his own transmission and dropped his truck on me. Come to think of it, the sounds are the same too. *Crap, I'm in the hospital again.* I seem to have an unnatural attraction to this place. Dammit, this time it wasn't even my fault.

Do they have to make those machines so friggin' noisy? I can't even hear myself think. It's absolutely insane. Between the incessant beeping and the sound of Jade arguing on the phone — Wait… Why is Jade here? I thought she was pissed off at me. I figured it would be a couple of months before she calmed down enough to be in my general presence. I try to lie still so I can quiet the sound of the blood rushing in my ears. I want to hear what Jade is saying.

Finally, I'm able to focus on her words as I watch her with her head bent to the side holding the phone in the crook of her neck as her hands are gesturing wildly. Wait! Why is she talking on *my* phone?

She's clearly trying to whisper, although her voice is quite loud, "Look, I'm sorry your niece didn't have someone to perform at her slumber party. I know; it sucked to be her." She pauses for a moment before continuing as she listens to the person on the other end of the phone. "Yes, I understand. I'm not making light of your situation. You don't understand, sir. Mr. Ailín made every effort to be there, but it was not possible."

This time, Jade holds my phone away from her ear and I can hear the muffled sounds of someone shouting through the phone even though I am several feet away from her. When the person on the other end of the phone finally runs out of breath, Jade responds, "I'd like to look at that written contract between you and Declan. I'd be interested to learn about the emergency provisions," she replies. When he answers in yet another angry tirade, she turns around to look at me and catches me watching her. She rolls her eyes in disgust as she waits for him to finish. When he does, she retorts, "So, what you're telling me is you and Mr. Ailín never had a contract for him to appear. He told you if he was free he would stop by and play a few songs, am I understanding correctly?" She pauses a few seconds before adding, "Yes, I understand he is living with you. Did he pay you any money for expenses? Was he late with his payment? Oh, I see — he wasn't late. Well, that's good." Jade continues to listen to the ongoing vitriolic word vomit.

She looks at me with wide eyes as she processes whatever this person said on the other end of the phone. She grabs a little notepad and pen from her purse as she suddenly asks, "What did you say your name was? Cornelius Tully?"

When I hear her say his name, I want to get out of bed and snatch the phone right out of her hand so she doesn't have to talk to the creep. I try to do exactly that. Inexplicably, I can't. I feel like I have zip ties strapping me into the bed. Jade sees me struggling and motions for me to stop.

Her body language tenses as she abruptly answers in the most professional voice I've heard her use so far, "I want to make sure I understand this: Declan isn't welcome to stay at your home anymore even though he's paid his rent because he wasn't able to sing at your niece's slumber party?"

After a few moments she spins around on the ball of her foot. "All right then. I understand." She shakes her head as she recants her statement, "No, that's not quite right, I *don't* understand. For the sake of politeness, I won't say more. I hope you do decide to take this to court. It would be fun to listen to you try to explain to a judge why you broke a perfectly solid rental agreement over a nonexistent contract when the reason he can't fulfill it is because he's in the hospital, but you're welcome to go ahead and be a jerk if you'd like. Someone will be by to get his things at five o'clock. Would it be helpful if you had FBI and DEA agents to supervise the packing? No? All right. Make sure none of his valuables are broken in the process of packing, please."

Jade pulls the phone away from her ear again as another barrage of words comes flying at her. Her eyes light up with fire as she hears the words being hurled in her general direction. The tone of her voice becomes lethal. "You need to check your tone. Mr. Ailín may have only been renting space in the corner of your basement and sleeping on your couch, but he was still your tenant. Fine, if you don't want us coming there, you can drop off his stuff at Ink'd Deep. Tell them Jade told you it was all right to put it in the back room."

I can't hear the next comment, but Jade's expression

darkens markedly as she replies, "No, if you had been paying attention at the beginning of this conversation when I introduced myself, you would know I was not some stripper Declan picked up at a street festival somewhere. I'm the co-owner of Ink'd Deep. If I wanted to, I could probably buy the house you're kicking Declan out of several times over. If I did, I wouldn't be a jerk and kick my tenant out because he ended up in the hospital. I happen to like being a decent human being, but whatever floats your boat. Have a good day, Mr. Tully."

Jade hangs up the phone and tosses it on the bed. She turns back to the window and shakes herself out like a sheepdog as she lets out a growl of frustration. Finally, she turns back around toward me.

"You might as well make me a list," Jade announces with a shrug.

"A list of what?" I ask blankly.

"I'm sure I'll have to replace nearly everything you own because I couldn't bring myself to be entirely polite to the cow-cud of a man who pretends to be your landlord. Where did you find this guy?"

"Cow-Cud?" I laugh even though it kills my bruised ribs.

Jade rolls her eyes so hard she can probably see the inside of her brain. "Whatever. I'm trying to make my dad happy. Even though we work at a tattoo place, my dad thinks it's bad for customer relations to have rough language. He instituted a swear-jar. At first it was funny, but then he upped the penalty. Don't get me wrong, I can afford it. It's the principle of the thing, I'm buying everybody lunch every week. I know Rogue swears as much as I do, but she does it in different languages and my dad doesn't catch her because it sounds all lyrical and poetic. I've been trying out new creative ways to say bad things about people. It's kind of therapeutic in a way. Anyway, I don't think you're getting your stuff back. This guy had egotistical, narcissistic jerk written all over him. He probably thinks he's entitled to your stuff as some sort of deposit for you staying there and breathing his air."

"Look, it's no huge loss. It's not like we were close or anything. He's a relative of a guy who sometimes plays keyboard with me on some of my larger venues. I barely knew him. He was trying to make extra cash to play online poker."

Jade smirks as she answers, "Figures. Did you have anything valuable at his house?"

I sink back against my pillows and close my eyes as the reality of last night hits me. My abrupt change in position knocks one of the sensors loose on my body and the alarm goes off, filling the room with a shrill, incessant noise that makes my head feel like it's going to explode any second. A nurse comes in and re-attaches the little sticker while giving Jade a serious case of stink eye. Jade is not having any of this and glares right back. The nurse glances back and forth between the two of us and advises pointedly, "You know, the hospital is a place to recover. You need to keep your activity to a minimum." She dramatically flounces from the room.

I look at Jade and comment, "It might be interesting to know what she thought we were doing in here."

Jade snorts. "I have an idea what she means, but I don't think you're quite up to those activities. Are you going to tell me what happened to you or do I have to guess by sorting through my nightmares?"

"To be honest, I'm not even sure I know the whole story. Eventually, I blacked out. I still have no idea how I got here for sure. I suppose Everett brought me."

"Who is Everett?"

"He's my unofficial busking partner. He drives a shuttle bus now, but back in the day he used to play saxophone in New Orleans, so he knows what I go through and he helps me out. I've got a round I do down by the outdoor restaurants by the campus at the University of Florida. If it's a rainy day and people aren't outside, I'll sometimes catch a ride on Everett's shuttle bus. I play a little guitar on the long stops. Everett says it makes the parents happy; a lot of times their kids are undergoing treatment at Shands. I don't make a lot of money on the Shands circuit, not like I do when I play downtown during a business convention or anything — but it's steady income; a few bucks here and there. Over time it adds up. There are a few people who live in the neighborhood who look forward to my arrival. There's this one college student who proofreads other people's term papers so she can afford to tip me. It's kinda cool to have a groupie of sorts."

"So, you were on the bus — but that doesn't add up to this," Jade insists, pointing at my broken hand.

"It was a quiet night and Everett was telling me about his kids' basketball game and how they hope to make the playoffs. We had a couple passengers to let off at the last stop before he put his bus to bed. He wanted to stop and get his boys a little something at Walmart before he went home so he was asking me what I thought would be a good present for a nine-year-old and an eleven-year-old. Then he remembered I don't have any kids and he was teasing me for being perpetually single. The lady on the bus was telling me she had a daughter with a great personality who would be a good match for me."

"Poor thing, you're a handsome rock star but you have to have little old ladies on the bus play matchmaker. I'm sorry, but that's too funny."

I don't even know what to say. I plow ahead with my story, "Anyway, everybody was in a great joking mood. The lady stood up to get off the bus and dropped a twenty in my guitar case while her husband got their bags. I helped her husband lift a heavy bag and make sure the handle was locked into place as we maneuvered it down the bus steps. When I turned back around to get back into my seat, someone blindsided me with a sucker punch. Someone else hit me with a metal pipe on my back and the back of my knees. As I struggled back to my feet, I could see them take all the money from my guitar case. That ticked me off because I had gotten a big tip and the rest of my night hadn't been terrible either. I couldn't figure out who these punks were because they didn't match the description of any one we had seen that night."

Jade scowls. "Maybe the bus has surveillance."

"I don't know, I'll have to ask Everett," I shudder at my memory. "They weren't your average teenage thugs. They must've had some training in fighting or something because the next thing I knew, this person was pummeling me in the face with rapid-fire punches. I'm not a professional by any means, but my brothers and I had a little karate and basic martial arts training when we were kids. My mom said with three boys, we had to have some sort of discipline or she'd go crazy."

"That's awful," Jade murmurs.

"I know there were two of them, but there's no way I shouldn't have been able to get a lick or two in. I haven't gotten my butt handed to me like this since about the sixth grade when I started growing my hair long and some older kids cornered me in the bathroom and decided I must be queer. They told me they were good church-going kids and felt the need to beat the gay out of me. I never forgot that beating, and I'll probably never forget this one either — or at least the parts of it I can remember."

I almost lose my nerve to finish the story as I watch Jade's emotional reaction to my words. It's almost as if she's reliving the fight. There is no sign of the legendary aloof Ice here. She is wearing every emotion on her face. "What did they want from you?" she asks in a tortured whisper.

"That was the weirdest part. It was eerily silent except for the sound of his punches and the pipe hitting my flesh. They weren't making any threats or calling me anything derogatory. They were systematically beating me to death for no apparent reason — it was almost like a sport or compulsion."

Jade shudders as she tries to regain her ability to speak. "What was the bus driver doing?" she probes, her voice full of indignation. "Shouldn't he have done something?"

I shake my head and then immediately regret the motion as the room starts to spin. It is then I remember some doctor I saw yesterday told me I had a severe concussion from the repeated hits on the back of my head from the metal pipe. "Everett was outside the shuttle with the couple who gave me the tip; the next thing I knew, I woke up here puking my guts out."

"What about those lousy carbon dioxide producers? What happened to them?" Jade demands.

The side of my mouth which isn't completely swollen quirks up. "That's not exactly what I would call them, but I don't know. The way my luck runs, they probably got away with my favorite guitar. I loved it too. It sounded sweet and fit me like a glove."

"I'm so sorry, Declan, that sucks. Then I had to go and make it worse by starting a pissing war with your friend," Jade twists her hair between her fingers.

"Jade, don't worry about it. The guy wasn't my friend. It was a place to hang my hat for a while. I'll find another place. Although it might be a little tricky right now. I doubt I'll be able to do my usual trick of staying in people's attics or in the loft above their garage. I don't think I'm up to climbing a bunch of stairs these days."

Our conversation is interrupted when a CNA comes in to take my vitals. It seems like she's been doing it every ten minutes since I woke up this morning. You should've seen how excited the medical staff was when I pooped. I haven't had anybody this interested in my bodily functions since I was about three and my mom used to give me stickers. Finally, when she finishes all of her paperwork, she announces, "Dr. Shelton said you would be able to go home this morning as long as your blood pressure is normal. You haven't shown any signs of further complications from your concussion, so we'll send you home with some instructions about how to monitor yourself. I assume you'll have someone with you, correct?"

Jade has resumed pacing in front of the hospital window; I can't see her very well because the medical technician is blocking my view from where I'm sitting in bed. The atmosphere in the room feels weird and I'm not sure what's going on. It almost feels like Jade and I should be arguing with each other, but we're not saying a word. I can't figure out what's going on and it's frustrating.

Finally, Jade walks over and stands in front of the CNA and she answers the question as if no time has passed instead of three or four minutes, "Yes, Mr. Ailín will be supervised. My home is a safe environment for him. His bedroom is downstairs so he won't have to navigate any stairs. I have safety equipment installed in my restroom because my grandparents used to live with me."

The CNA looks at Jade with admiration. "My, you certainly have put a lot of thought into this. That sounds ideal." She turns to me. "I assume you have no objection to this plan? Most folks are itching to get out of here by now. Our food leaves a bit to be desired."

Before the part of my brain which actually has common sense kicks in, the part of my brain which rules my heart answers. "Sure, sounds like a solid plan to me."

CHAPTER FIVE

JADE

EVER SINCE I WAS a small child, I've always had conversations with myself in my head. Onyx used to think this was so weird. When I was in the first grade, he totally had me convinced I had a twin who was stuck behind my bellybutton and my blood vessels were like a telephone line to my brain. I completely believed him for more years than I want to admit.

The voice in my head is having a full-on argument with my soft and gullible heart right now.

I have to admit, the "What the heck were you thinking?" camp started winning from the moment I catch my new kitten, Inkblot, playing with a tampon from the box I left out on the bathroom counter this morning. He is currently chasing it across the floor like it's the best cat toy he's ever seen. The shiny, hot pink wrapper is like a neon sign announcing, "Hey, a chick lives here!"

A chick *does* live here. A chick who wasn't even remotely expecting to bring a guy home. He'll definitely get a look at the unfiltered version of Jade. He has only seen me at work and in carefully orchestrated social environments, and my work facade is organized. Okay, that's kind of the understatement of the century. I am extremely regimented at work — we all have to be.

In the tattoo business you must be clean beyond reproach. It's one of the things Ink'd Deep is known for. When I come home, I'm not afraid to let my inner slob run free. My habit affects no one except me — usually. I try to discreetly hide a large laundry basket full of underwear and bras which is sitting on the guest bed as I escort a very shaky, sleepy Declan to his new quarters.

At first, I thought I had gotten away with my habit of using my whole guest room as a huge oversized dresser because Declan seems out of it as I cover him with a large blanket and adjust his pillows. As I flip off the light and leave the room, I hear him mumble, "The pretty panties are nice."

I can hear Declan snoring as I stand in front of my refrigerator surveying its pathetic contents. What do I feed the poor man? He probably won't like my constant diet of cheap TV dinners much. I know I could afford more now, but they are like a comfort food for me now. I kind of like some of them and it seems stupid to pay more for food when I don't need to. I live by myself. I don't have to impress anyone and nobody cares if I eat food from boxes with pictures of dinner on the front. It's just easier. I feel foolish as I look at the shelves. It's not as if I don't know how to cook, because I do. I'm not as good as Mama Rosa, but then again, few people are. My Grandma Dimitra taught my brother and me to cook when we went to stay with her during the summer. It breaks my heart a little to cook without him. It was a hobby we shared and my kitchen feels empty without him in it.

At least I've gotten the rest of the house in decent shape while Declan's been sleeping. I feel a bit better about my decision now. At least there's less to embarrass myself over now. I still wonder what he'll think of the place. I rarely invite people over because seeing my home is like a window into who I really am on the inside. Most people see a cartoon version of me based on the person I am at the shop, dance club or when I'm out performing karaoke. Yet, none of those public, social personas reflect who I truly am. Part of me wonders if I even remember who I am at the core. With Onyx gone, I sometimes forget which Jade is the real one and which is the one created for public consumption. He was always my reality check.

I take a deep breath and try to shake off my maudlin mood as I walk over to the pantry and check its admittedly scarce contents. I smile a tiny grin of victory when I spot a couple of boxes of shell pasta. Thanks to my grandma, I can make a mean batch of macaroni and cheese. There's something to be said for having both African-American and Greek heritage. We do comfort food like nobody's business.

As I put the casserole in the oven, I hear a loud stream of cussing coming from the back of the house. *Crap! I didn't even hear him get out of bed.* Declan was supposed to call me if he needed help. I take off at a dead sprint to the back of the house, scaring Inkblot half to death as I almost fall over when I try to avoid stepping on his tail.

I head directly toward the guest bedroom because that's where I left Declan. As soon as I pass the bathroom, it becomes abundantly clear I need to go no further. It sounds like I've trapped a herd of elephants in there. After another long, creative tirade of colorful words erupts from Declan, I knock on the bathroom door and ask politely, "Is everything okay in there? Should I send in some sort of rescue team? Tristan and Isaac specialize in those, you know," I quip. "Mitch even has dogs which could find you. I think he's here doing a seminar with Isaac and Tristan."

"Very funny!" snaps Declan. "It's not like I don't know how to dress myself, I just can't because of this stupid cast."

"I can see how it would be tricky," I sympathize, trying to keep my voice even. It's hard not to laugh at his predicament; he looks like a four-year-old whose favorite balloon has blown away at the fair. Before I can stop to think of the ramifications, I offer, "You want some help?"

Declan looks down at himself as his hair flops limply in his face. "I don't know what you could do, my jeans are too tight for me to button with one hand. They are the kind with buttons on the fly. It took me next to forever to get them undone, I may have ripped out a buttonhole."

I study Declan for a few moments before making an impulsive offer, "How do you feel about purple?"

Declan wrinkles his nose at me as he responds, "You know I'm from Florida, right? It's sacrilege to ask a Heat fan to wear purple. Lucky for you I also like the Saints."

I stick my tongue out at him as I blow a raspberry. "Geez, you're as bad as Onyx. I don't care much about sports unless I'm winning money off Marcus in the shop pool. To be honest, I choose the winning team by which starter has the prettiest eyes."

I laugh at Declan as he gasps in dismay. "Oh, please!

It's not as if your method is any more scientific. Anyway, my preferences in sweats are based solely on comfort and not team loyalty, so you would be betraying no one."

I watch as he sizes me up skeptically. "I know I wear my hair long and all, but last I checked I'm still a guy and you're still a girl —"

Despite my best intentions, I can't stop my eyes from settling on his open fly as he says those words and my face heats. "I'm aware," I bluff as I try to gain my composure. "It won't be a problem because I wear my sweats several sizes too big. They arc for lounging around the house and I like being comfortable. Even my dad can wear them and you know how big he is. We found that out the hard way a couple years ago when he fell into my pool."

"Wow, your dad is bigger than me. Your dad is bigger than most folks. Are you sure you don't mind?"

I shake my head. "Of course not. It'll be several minutes before dinner is through cooking. Why don't you take a shower? I'll get you some clean clothes to wear while we wait for dinner."

"I think I'd like that. Hospital funk is worse than road trip funk. I'm not sure how to keep this thing dry though. The doc said there are some stitches under the cast and it would be gnarly if I got it wet," he explains, holding up his hand.

I have to bite my lip to keep from laughing. "I think one of the Teenage Mutant Ninja Turtles called and asked for their slang back," I tease.

"What do you want from me, Ice? I'm tired. It's been a long day, and honestly, I feel like I been run over by a truck."

Immediately, I feel guilty for making fun of him. "Be right back with a plastic bag, your clothes and some towels," I yell as I run down the hall. I return and stack the stuff on the counter as I comment, "I'll be down in the kitchen if you need anything."

I usually make my grandma's carrot salad when I have macaroni and cheese; I decide it might not be such a great option with Declan's sore jaw. An idea strikes me as I remember the huge fruit basket my parents gave me. The other day, the bananas were green, but today they should be about perfect. I sprint to my pantry and hope I've stashed all the ingredients I need. I haven't made this in a while. It used to be one of Onyx's favorite dishes and secretly it's one of my favorite comfort foods. I drag a kitchen chair over and stand on it so I can reach to the very far back corner of the highest cupboard in my kitchen. I have to catch my breath as I see a familiar yellow box with red letters. I can't open a box of these without remembering Onyx teaching me to count using these silly vanilla wafers. More often than not it usually ended up with him eating my cookies and telling me I needed to learn to count faster if I wanted to keep up with him.

I grab the Jell-O pudding mix from the pantry. That was always another bone of contention between us — I prefer this dish made with the vanilla pudding, but Onyx was old-school and wanted his fixed with banana pudding if I could find it in the grocery store. I have one box of banana pudding left — it's probably hopelessly out of date and not even safe to use, but I've never been able to bring myself to throw it away. I was planning to fix it for Onyx when he came home for the holidays, but never got the chance. Swallowing hard, I gently place the box of banana pudding in its traditional spot in the pantry and mix the vanilla pudding with some milk and set it aside while I clean up the crystal bowl my grandma gave me; it has a little pedestal on it which makes even this little humble dish look grand.

It's odd cooking my favorite food for someone else, but I feel a little ball of happiness glowing in my chest as I peel and slice up the bananas and arrange them in the bowl with the cookies, pudding and whipped cream. I come scarily close to slicing my finger when the floor above me shakes and there is a loud crash. I set the food aside and give my hands a quick rinse under the kitchen faucet. I dry them off and go upstairs at a dead run. I'm almost afraid to open the bathroom door. I'm a tall woman, but Declan is still larger than me. I take my cell phone out of my pocket and get ready to dial 911 because I'm not sure what awaits me.

I knock softly on the door before asking, "Is it okay if I come in?"

"Go ahead," Declan's snarls, "it's not as if everything isn't already screwed up anyway."

Almost holding my breath with trepidation, I peek around the door not knowing what to expect. The sight before me is both comical and heartbreaking. Declan is sitting on the edge of the tub, trying to hold a sopping wet towel around his midsection and his beautiful long hair is flowing around his shoulders in wet ringlets, half covered in soap. Even the plastic wrapping I helped him so carefully apply to his injured arm is somewhat askew.

Before I can even begin to apply a politeness filter, the words come flying out of my mouth, "Oh honey! You are in some serious need of help. You are a hot mess."

Declan scowls at me. "You think? I practically

launched myself through your shower enclosure. They told me at the hospital I'd be a little shaky, but I didn't think I would be this weak. I am a full-grown man — I should be able to stand long enough to get a shower. This is freakin' ridiculous. All I wanted to do was get clean. What kind of weakling can't even stand up?"

"First of all, nobody ever said you were a weakling. Secondly, you recently had the crap beat out of you. You're not weak, you're recuperating — that's different. The only reason you got out of the hospital was because I promised to take care of you. You need to let me."

"That's the other thing, I'm supposed to be earning your affections, not making more work for you. It's not as if you don't have enough stuff to do at the shop."

I sigh as I grab my swimming bag off the hook on the back of the door. "Dec, most times I don't mind verbally sparring with you, but this time you need to stick a sock in it and let me help you. Sit tight for a bit and I'll be right back."

When I come back into the bathroom, Declan lets out a long moan and I regret my decision to take the time to change into a bathing suit. I should've crawled into the shower wearing my clothes. I hate wearing wet jeans. "Hop in the shower, let's get this show on the road before dinner gets cold," I instruct as I check the water temperature. I jump into the shower and extend my hand for him to hold.

A pained expression crosses Declan's face. "Are you sure this is a good idea?"

"Sure it is," I fix the plastic bag over his cast and refasten the tape. "I told you I used to take care of my grandparents all the time. I'm good at this kind of stuff."

Declan groans. "Something tells me it won't exactly be the same."

I shrug. "Dec, I'm not exactly known for playing by the rules, so whatever happens, happens. It's pointless to worry about it right now. You're about to collapse where you stand. Please let me take care of you. We'll sort it all out later."

I can tell when he gives up the fight. Usually when we spar, it's for fun and it's usually about something lighthearted and stupid. I think one of the last arguments we had was over which flavor of ice cream was the best. The one before that was over whether Coke or Pepsi was the preferable brand of cola. When we argued over the correct way to hang up toilet paper, the argument went on so long I finally had to settle it with the original patent illustration. In all the years we've been friends, I've never known him to acquiesce quite so quickly. Usually, there's quite a bit more teasing involved and at least a few more rounds of protest votes at least. As I take a moment to study him, his bruises stand out against his pale skin even more than they did this morning and although the swelling has gone down a little around his eye, it still looks extremely painful. He looks shaky and frail. It is not a look I associate with him at all.

Cautiously, I help him step over the side of the tub. I stand him in front of the shower head as I duck around him and grab the handheld shower wand. Living alone, this garden tub always seemed a little excessive, but I'm beginning to see its benefits since I can freely move around Declan. I put some of my shower gel on a sponge and start to wash his back and his arms. I can feel his muscles flex under the sponge. I take a second to appreciate the power and symmetry. This is a little disconcerting, although I didn't expect it to be. I touch guys all the time. It's part of my job. In fact, I've touched *Declan* in some intimate places, but it's never been quite like this. It's almost as if there is some weird electrical current sparking between us. I must be imagining things because we've never taken our relationship there before. Sure, sometimes we make jokes with each other about our dating status, but it's never been serious.

Shaking my head, I try to get my head back in the game and concentrate on what I'm supposed to be paying attention to. I kneel on the bottom of the tub and wash his legs. As I make my way up toward his thighs, he makes a slight choking sound. "I've got it from here."

"You sure?" I ask as I stand up.

Declan closes his eyes tightly and clutches the wet towel at his waist as he nods. "I'm fine."

I look around the bathtub enclosure until I find the bottle I'm looking for and I grab it as I order, "Lean down a little so I can wash your hair."

Declan rolls his eyes. "I suppose I get to smell like roses or baby powder all day or something."

The corner of my mouth turns up. "I suppose that could be arranged if you'd like. I have a ton of different kinds of shampoo, but I like this particular one because it smells like pine trees at Christmas."

"That's macho of you. I'm impressed. I thought you might be all about girly stuff. I've seen some of your shoes, remember?"

"Like I told you, I'm not a big follower of arbitrary rules," I quip. When I reach up to wash his hair and massage his scalp with my fingertips, he makes a sound which can only be described as a male purr. He opens his good eye suddenly as if he's in shock he let his guard down enough to allow anything to slip out.

"Sorry," he mumbles.

"It's all right, relax and let me help you. You'll get used to it."

"That's what I'm afraid of," Declan confesses as he leans his head back against my shoulder.

Chapter Six

Declan

I'VE HEARD OF THINGS being simultaneously heaven and hell, but I've never related to that concept so closely until now. If it hadn't been for the hospital incessantly calling my cell phone to check on me to make sure I made it home, our shower would've ended very differently. As fate would have it, earlier today, while Jade was in the pharmacy getting my medication, I was bored and I reprogrammed all the ringtones on my phone and I assigned the hospital an ambulance siren for a ring tone. While I was amused when I did it, it was not so amusing when things got hot-n-heavy in the shower. I was about to move in for some serious kissing and my phone went berserk. Talk about your complete mood killer.

I thought I had pulled myself together pretty well and was acting like a relatively normal human being, but things went way off track again at dinnertime. I'm still not sure exactly what went wrong. I was having a blast discovering Jade's hidden talents as a cook. I honestly didn't know she knew how to do anything except heat up hot pockets in the microwave. That's the only thing I've ever seen her eat. I thought she subsisted entirely on TV dinners and energy drinks. I'm shocked to learn she has mad culinary skills. She insists she's not so great, but she cooks better than anybody I know. My mom is decent, but nothing like Jade. My mom taught my brothers and me just enough so we don't burn the house down. Beyond that, I wouldn't call us gifted. I can grill decent steaks on the barbecue, but I wouldn't win any contests at the firehouse. I'm supposed to be taking it easy for a couple of weeks because my attackers did serious damage and I've got some bruised ligaments the doctors want to heal before I put them under any substantial stress.

Everything seemed to be going okay until we started talking about Jade's movie collection and she brought out a dessert. More precisely, I was arguing with her about whether she would let me add a bunch of premium channels to her cable package while I'm staying here. As soon as I saw the Nilla wafer dessert, I made some stupid, off-hand remark, "Sweet! I used to make it all the time with my brother, Finn."

Jade abruptly dissolved into tears. Her reaction completely stuns me. I've seen Jade in some stressful situations, but I've never seen her burst into tears. I have been present when Jett dressed her down in front of customers in a way which would send me crying for my mom and I've heard customers at the shop say vile and nasty things to her that made me want to bawl or punch someone. Fortunately, their behavior earned them a lifetime ban from Ink'd Deep. Even through it all, I've never seen her like this. I guided her over to the couch and leaned her back against my chest, ignored my tender ribs as she finally relaxed into me and started telling me about the painful memories involving her brother, Onyx.

I feel absolutely helpless. There isn't anything I can do to help or make the situation better. Her brother is gone and I can't fix it for her. Unfortunately, I can't bring him back. Sadly, I didn't know him. He must've already gone away to college when I got my first tattoo from Jett. All I can do is try to guess the type of person he was by the imprint he left behind on the people I care about. The size of the crater left in Jade's life is understandably huge.

She had a relationship with her brother I wish I had with mine. Finn and Rowan are okay as far as brothers go, but nobody would be making any mushy greeting cards about us either. Everything is competitive beyond belief in my family. Who can rack up the most customer contacts? Who can sell the most cars? Who can sell the most warranties? Who can bring in the most customers? Who can shake the most hands in a day? That's what was discussed at my dinner table when I was growing up. It's been part of my family's doctrine from before we could speak for ourselves. Before my brothers and I could form our own friendship bonds, we were made to compete with each other. I never felt like I had their support, especially when I decided I wanted to break away from the family and determine my own path in life. That isn't done in my family. Everyone is expected to branch out and start a new family car lot. It is what you do when you have my last name. Only, it's not what I wanted to do. Making that decision has cost me nearly everyone I love.

Although, as I look at Jade dozing on my chest, I realize how unfair my own thoughts are. As annoying and overpowering as my family is, it would only take a few very awkward and condescending phone calls for me to be back in touch with them. We seem to be at an impasse at the moment because no one seems to know how to make the first move. Unfortunately, Jade and her family don't have the option. Onyx is forever gone.

Hearing how the suicide of her brother permeates every facet of Jade's life makes me contemplate what it would be like if my family was truly absent from mine. Over the last few years I've tried to connect with my family, but it usually ends up being a huge train wreck with things more messed up than when I started. I began to stay away from my family entirely. It seems less painful that way.

After listening to all of Jade's stories, I wonder if my approach is really less painful for everyone. If I'm honest with myself, I miss my mom a lot. Sometimes, I wonder how much she misses me. I hope she isn't in as much pain as Jade. I never set out to break my mom's heart. I simply wanted to be my own person.

Jade becomes restless and shifts in her sleep. She inadvertently elbows me and it's all I can do to not jump off the couch as she hits one of my fractured ribs. As I suck in a deep breath, I glance down at her and notice a tear trailing down her cheek. I whisk it away with the pad of my thumb. Jade mumbles in her sleep and moves toward the heat of my hand as she snuggles closer and tangles her fingers in my hair. Yep, this is like walking a tightrope between heaven and hell. For years I have dreamed of holding Jade like this. These are so *not* the circumstances under which I wanted something like this to happen. As I raise my other hand to stroke her hair, I am rudely reminded nothing says romance like a fiberglass cast.

Two things hit me at once when I wake up. First, Jade isn't with me anymore and secondly, at some point during the night, somebody must've come in and broken every single bone in my body and tried to pry my face off with a crowbar. What in the freak happened to me? I hurt so bad I need to hurl — *oh crap, I need to puke.* I can't even move. "Jade!" I bellow as I try to take a deep breath and stave off the inevitable.

She runs into the living room wearing a microscopically short bathrobe and a towel on her head "Sorry, I was hoping to get a shower while you were still asleep," Jade remarks as she comes around the corner of the couch. As soon as she sees my expression, she stops dead in her tracks. "I'm an idiot, I let you get behind on your pain medication and now you're a mess. I don't know what happened last night. I guess I shouldn't have started talking about Onyx — but, that's my problem, not yours. You have enough pain going on, I didn't need to add to it. Even worse, I used you as a pillow even though I knew you were sore. Some Florence Nightingale I am."

I try to explain it wasn't her fault, but as soon as I open my mouth, a wave of nausea overtakes me. I have to stop and start breathing funny again. Jade must have read my expression because she grabs a plant off of the side table by the couch and removes it from the decorative galvanized bucket. She hands me the bucket and says, "I'll be back with a cool washcloth and some 7-Up."

"I don't want to ruin your stuff," I croak between breaths. I absolutely hate to throw up. When I was little, Finn used to tell me if I threw up, it was because all the souls who couldn't find a place to live in your body were escaping so they could inhabit someone else. I suppose on a certain level, part of me might still believe him.

Jade rolls her eyes at me. "It's a bucket from the discount store, it can be replaced. You're tossing your cookies, not spewing nuclear waste or anything."

Another wave of nausea hits and I have to hunch over the bucket and as usual, my mop of hair is being a gargantuan pain in the ass. Realizing a colossal mess is imminent I angrily try to tuck it behind my ear, but it's not very effective. I feel Jade's cool hand on my shoulder as she suggests, "Let me take care of that for you."

To be honest, between my colossal shiner and my current headache and nausea, I'm having trouble focusing on the world around me and I can't figure out what she's doing. Apparently, she has a hairband around her wrist and she is gathering my hair up into a ponytail.

"Better?" Jade asks when she completes her task.

Instinctively I nod. It was the very last straw. I let loose with a scene reminiscent of some horror movie. I haven't been this sick since Finn and Rowan persuaded me to drink green beer when I was about nine. When I finally finish my personal exorcism, I feel about as steady as a newborn. It seems as if every bit of blood has rushed out of my upper torso and down to my feet. I feel shaky and cold. I close my eyes and rest against the back of the couch. I don't know how long I lay there before I hear Jade suggest, "You might feel better if you rinse your mouth out."

I struggle to open my good eye and focus. Wow, I must've been out longer than I thought I was, because now Jade is wearing one of those little romper things with a big floral pattern which always makes me think she would be right at home on a Hawaiian island somewhere. She is holding out a tray with my toothbrush, toothpaste and a cup of water with a dish to spit in.

Ironically, my body chooses that very second to wake

the rest of the way up and more pressing needs take over. I look up at her with a startled look on my face as I blurt, "It's nice of you. But right now, I desperately need to take a pee. The only problem is, I hurt so bad I'm not even sure I can walk. I think I should've stayed in the hospital. I don't even know how to handle taking a piss right now."

Much to her credit, Jade doesn't even look fazed by my awkward announcement. She merely sets the tray down and proclaims, "From my experience, it's best to approach this stuff one step at a time. If you can't make it, I can get you an old coffee can to pee in."

I consider myself a worldly guy. After all, I'm a street performer. I've seen pretty much everything. I routinely perform at clothing optional Renaissance Fairs, but the idea of relieving myself in a coffee can and needing Jade to take care of that for me is a little too much, even for me. I blush bright red as I stammer, "No, I think I'd like to try going to the restroom on my own. I'm a big boy — or, at least I was a few days ago. Now I'm not so sure."

"Declan, you were beaten to the point of unconsciousness. It is a miracle you weren't more seriously hurt. Stop worrying about trying to impress me. At this point, I'm impressed you're still breathing. I've cleaned up a lot worse stuff than puke in my lifetime. Get over it."

I give her a mock salute, forgetting about my bad hand, "Crap, this is going to be a long recovery," I mutter to myself.

Jade grins at me as she quips, "Buck up, Buttercup. Look at it this way; at least you're not standing on a street corner busking. It's pouring down rain." She turns the television on and flips through the channels. After pausing on the guide channel for a few moments she exclaims, "Oh look! There's a *Rocky* marathon starting in about thirty minutes. That ought to keep you busy for a while. Let's get you up so I can make you some breakfast," she cajoles as she helps pull me to a standing position.

I'm not exactly sure what to say. I'm almost positive I didn't tell her I had Sylvester Stallone posters on my wall as a kid — I'm certain she wouldn't find it overly impressive.

Fortunately, my wake-up calls the next couple of mornings are a little less eventful. Being this dependent on someone isn't getting any easier. I can't remember sleeping this much since I was a teenager. The last time I was this exhausted, I was in the eighth grade and all three of us got mono. I'm still amazed my mom survived it all. My brothers and I were cranky for a couple of months straight — she must've thought she was going insane.

I'm getting stir crazy already. It's funny how when you get something you've always wished for, it doesn't seem to be what you thought it would be. A lot of people think being a street musician is an easy gig. I can understand why they draw that conclusion because I'm free to go where I want to go and see the people I want to see. I don't check in with a particular boss and if I don't like my coworkers, I can go work somewhere else. Those are the things I like about what I do. What people don't see is how incredibly hard I work. I do have to keep a regular schedule; my tips are better when people can expect me to be at a certain place, at a certain time. If coffee shops, restaurant owners and fair organizers can count on me to be around, they're more likely to invite me to play for them again. That reduces the risk for me as a musician. If I don't have to go into a strange neighborhood, I know I'm not busking in anyone else's territory and throwing shade on anyone else. I usually try not to overlap with anyone else's corner or take someone else's tips.

I have been doing this long enough that my area has grown pretty large and I spend a crap-load of time on the road. I often fantasize about having enough free time to sit around and watch TV and read all the books I could find. Yet, now that I've had several days of sitting around watching television and reading, I hardly know what to do with myself. This is not enough for me. I used to think I was the kind of person who could lie around and do nothing. Clearly, I am not. I have so much pent up energy. I am about to burst. I've tried to get up and pace, but I can't do that either. Jade took me to my follow-up appointment yesterday with the doctor and they explained the results of the MRI of my knee and my ankle. There is some extensive tendon and ligament damage caused by the strike from the pipe.

It's weird, I could tell the doctor exactly how the pipe hit me to cause the damage, I remember the searing hot pain and the odd squishy, tearing sound coming from my knee joint. The damage to my ankle is a little more of a mystery, but I still recall them hitting it viciously before I passed out. They must have broken my hand when I was trying to hold on to my guitar. It still ticks me off that they felt they could take everything from me. I don't know how I'll replace it, although I'm not sure what good it would do. The doctors don't even know if there's any lasting nerve damage to my fingers. They are a little concerned about the numbness in my thumb. They took my cast off and put a new one on to see if it was due to the position of my hand. Much to my frustration, the new cast is not any more flexible than the old one and it still interferes with almost everything.

At least I'm able to operate Jade's coffee machine. She doesn't seem to be up yet this morning, so I'm trying to fix her some breakfast. It is freakin' hard to crack eggs with my left hand and get them into the skillet without cracking the yolks. I finally give up and decide to scramble the eggs. I look in the refrigerator for some cheese. I groan out loud when I finally find it. Why can't she buy the pre-shredded kind in the bag like all the rest of us? I start opening her drawers to find her cheese grater. Cooking in someone else's kitchen is strange. Fortunately, I get lucky and find it in the third drawer. It's a box grater, so it stands up on its own. That's lucky for me — I don't know what I would've done if I would've had to balance it on a bowl. I'm concentrating so hard on grating cheese I almost forget to stir the eggs. Crap! I forgot toast. When in the world did a simple breakfast of scrambled eggs and toast become as complicated as an Olympic sport? This is crazy!

I don't even notice when Jade enters the kitchen. She walks up quietly behind me and reaches around me and grabs a couple of plates as she asks, "Need a hand?"

I do the unmanly thing right there in her kitchen and I scream like a ninny, "Oh Geez, I didn't see you there!"

Jade raises her eyebrow. "That's rather obvious. Good morning, Declan. How are you this morning? Breakfast smells delicious. Do you need some salt and pepper on these eggs?"

I smack my forehead with my good hand. "Yes, they need seasoning. It's a good thing you came down to rescue me or your breakfast would've been almost completely inedible."

"Oh, I doubt it. I just take a little salt with mine. It's not like Ivy and Rogue. You don't want to know what those two do to eggs — you don't put habañero sauce on yours do you?" she asks.

"No, last I checked, I wasn't insane. I use my voice for a living. I need my vocal cords. Regular, good old-fashioned table salt and pepper is enough for me."

Jade looks around the kitchen and sees the cheese. "Oh good, you grated a ton of cheese. That's the way I like mine too."

She dumps the cheese in the skillet and seasons the eggs before she turns the eggs out onto the plates. She pulls some bread out from her breadbox and inquires, "Light, medium or dark?"

"Medium is fine, thank you."

"Perfect, I don't even have to change the toaster. Go sit down at the table and I will bring you your toast and coffee when it's done."

"How do you know how I take my coffee?"

"You're kidding, right? I've known you forever — you take two sugars and one Splenda. I'm not sure what your reasoning is, but whatever. Everybody has a preference."

"I don't know, the Splenda seems super-sweet to me. I feel like it turbo boosts the caffeine in my coffee or something. Mixing the fake and the real stuff seems like it creates the perfect balance."

"Or something is right," Jade retorts with a smirk. "I don't even want to think about how many lab rats died while they were developing it. You could be petrifying your insides."

"Says the woman who eats fake brown gravy on virtually everything. I don't think you have much room to talk. I didn't even know you knew how to use any appliances other than the microwave," I counter.

Jade walks over and hands me a steaming cup of coffee and then toasts me with her cup. "Touché, I can respect a man who makes a good point. Here's to making new discoveries about each other."

She takes a long sip of her coffee and sighs. "You know, I could get entirely too used to having you around. I like the coffee when you make it."

Hmm… Two can play this game. I wonder how honest I can be without flinching. I attempt to act casual as I comment, "It's nice to be able to watch the games live."

Jade shrugs. "It's nice to have help with the crossword puzzle."

"It's cool to have Wi-Fi. My cell phone reception isn't great," I concede.

"I sleep well with you in the house," she counters.

"It is nice to have someone to talk to. If I talk to myself on the bus, people think I'm crazy."

"I like having someone to cook for. Turns out my food tastes better than TV dinners."

"Well, duh!" I exclaim as I eat a few more bites of eggs and toast. "You're a great cook; I don't know why you don't brag about it more."

The teasing grin disappears from Jade's face for a moment as she goes quiet. "I guess cooking was always a fun family activity for me but everyone I always cooked with is gone and it seems like such a huge bother to do it for just me. Without my grandma and Onyx, there doesn't seem to be much point in going through the ritual. The whole point of cooking was to see the joy on someone else's face. It's pointless if I'm cooking for one. I might as well eat from a box."

"I like being the person you cook for. I like it a lot. I like that you go out of your way to make me happy," I admit more than I probably intended to.

Jade glances away from me and starts to stack the plates on the table before she clears her throat. "It's weird. Most of the time people notice when I'm being outrageous or inappropriate. It's not very often somebody pays attention to the little stuff I do. I've made a reputation for being edgy and out there. Sometimes it's hard for people to see beyond that and understand it's not who I really am." She stops and runs her fingers through her hair and shakes it out before she continues, "That's not quite right. There are parts of me which are the wild and crazy over-the-top Jade everyone thinks I am. I like that part of me too, but it's not all me. I wish everybody could see that as well as you do. I swear my dad still sees me as the rebellious fourteen-year-old who tried to pierce my own septum by flashlight. I'm not that kid anymore."

"Jade, I think every parent struggles to recognize their child has grown up. I think Jett will come around. I know I like both the loud public side of you and the quieter side."

Jade looks a little startled by my confession, but the corner of her mouth turns up as she softly declares, "I like you a lot more than I expected to as well. I thought you were more like an overgrown surfer without a lot of drive and purpose. I guess I misread you."

"I think there's a lot of that going on, I had

preconceptions about you too," I sheepishly reply.

A positively evil grin crosses Jade's face as she challenges, "Care to share? This could be both entertaining and *very* informative—"

I nearly choke on my coffee when I think of all the different directions my thoughts have traveled when it comes to Jade. I make a gesture pretending to zip my lips. "I think I will take a pass on your offer on the grounds I might incriminate myself. I think we've done enough sharing for now. I'm happy here and I don't want to do anything to upset you, so you feel compelled to kick me out. I can't deny I've got a bit of wanderlust going on. I would give anything to have my lyric notebook and my guitar right about now. I've got songs tumbling around in my head and no way to pull them out and put them down on paper. It's so frustrating."

Jade opens her mouth, but no sound comes out for a moment. She tries again after she clears her throat and blinks away tears. "I think I can help you with that."

CHAPTER SEVEN

JADE

"I'M GLAD TO SEE you could finally drag your butt to work." My dad passes by me in the office.

I fight to keep my expression neutral. "Dad, I wasn't even gone a whole week. You know Declan was seriously hurt. The hospital didn't want him to be left alone. He has no one else. He trusted me enough to let me take care of him. Doesn't that count for something?"

My dad scoffs. "Yeah, I bet he did. I bet you guys had a great time playing 'doctor'. Meanwhile, the rest of us were responsible for carrying your weight while you were off flouncing around. Your brother would've never done something like that to me."

I gasp out loud. I can't believe he said those words. I pick up my phone and send Marcus and Rogue a text message, "Lunch — taking Dad."

Trying to catch my breath and keep my cool, I grab my sweater off the back of my office chair and take my dad by his arm and escort him out the back door of the shop.

"Where are we going?" he protests. "I have work to do. So do you since you've been lollygagging around."

When we are clear of the shop and the main parking lot, I walk him over to my car and open the door. Fortunately, I parked in the overflow lot this morning and there is no one around. "Unlike you, I don't like to air our private business in front of all the customers. You and I need to have a conversation in private. Probably a lengthy one, because it's been percolating for a while, but I've had enough."

"You're my daughter, you don't get to talk to me that way," my dad grouses. "You should have more respect."

"Respect is a two-way street. You have to respect me too. I am one-third owner of this business, but you don't talk to me about business decisions like you do with Marcus. Instead, you talk about me in front of the customers and it's humiliating."

"If you're one-third owner of this business, then you better step up and take over your part of the business. You've been slacking off like you don't care about what happens to Ink'd Deep. I don't know what's happened to you since your brother's death, but you don't act like you even want to be here."

"Dad! That's ridiculous," I answer, shock making my voice sound shaky. "I care so much about Ink'd Deep, you don't even know. I have worked at this business for as long as I can remember. I've practically been an employee of this business since I don't know — the first grade? I knew how to trace designs on the light box before most kids understood how to color in a coloring book. While most kids were learning what a nickel looks like, I knew how to make change for a hundred and how to run the cash register. Do *not* tell me I don't care about this business."

"Then why are you taking time off to play hanky-panky with the rock star?" my dad argues.

"For the last time, I wasn't on vacation with Declan — I was taking care of him. You don't understand how badly he was beaten. It's lucky he didn't come away with a traumatic brain injury. They took after him with a metal pipe."

"Let's say I buy your story about the boy. You've been acting strange for a while. The other day, I saw you start a tat and not finish it. What's up with that crap? We don't do that around here. You didn't make that kind of mistake, even when you were a rookie."

"Dad, trust me. It was not a mistake. I did it on purpose. I am well aware it was not professional behavior, and if there are consequences arising from it, I will take them on personally. The customer was nasty to her core and I could not allow her to disrespect the memory of my brother for sport. It was better for my psyche to pay her to go away."

"Why did you drive her friends away too?" my dad counters, his voice getting louder with every syllable. "They had tattoos booked that day. You know, we need business in order for the shop survive. We have employees to pay, rent to cover and supplies to buy."

This time, I don't even bother to disguise my frustration as I roll my eyes. "Do you think I don't know that? I've been helping with payroll and inventory since I was about thirteen years old."

"Then why did you let perfectly good customers walk?" he probes, his tone condescending.

"I don't remember you questioning Marcus this much on the way he handles customers," I observe dryly.

"Maybe that's because he uses the good sense his

mama gave him," my dad answers in a huff.

"I use my sense fine, Dad. If you can't trust me to know what I'm doing, maybe you need to find another partner," I finally answer with profound sadness.

My dad looks as if I've slapped him. I can't say I blame him. I'm shocked I said those words out loud. "You want out?" he stammers. "Because I asked you why you went on vacation?" He lifts his heavy ponytail from his neck and tightens the leather thong holding his hair. "I never thought I'd see the day that you were a bigger drama queen than your mother."

"Stop. This has nothing to do with being a drama queen or going on vacation — although I am seriously due for one. Even when my friends got married in Paris, I was only there for two days. What sane person does that?"

"What is this about then?" he asks exasperated.

"Dad, I'm working on keeping a promise I made to Onyx a long time ago."

"Don't you bring your dead brother's name into this like it's a justification for doing such a cowardly thing. He already did that once. Just because he was too weak to live his life doesn't mean you get to use it as an excuse to give up all I've built for you. Are you a Petros or are you turning your back on that too?"

"Daddy! You have no idea what Onyx lived through or why he made his decision. We can only speculate whether it had anything to do with us or the shop or why in the heck he did it. All we have are those few precious words he left in the note — and hundreds of thousands of guesses and nightmares and the conversations we play over and over in our heads. The one thing we cannot do is put ourselves in Onyx's shoes, because we were not there. We don't know what was happening to him in that moment when he decided to end it all. We can't pretend we were. It is not fair for you to call him weak. You can call me all the names you want to if it makes you feel better. Go ahead, take all the verbal punches you can. Leave Onyx out of it because he is not here to defend himself ..." I let my speech trail off as my anger boils over and I'm left with nothing but a gaping hole of sadness where my brother once was. I can't control my sobs. I'm crying so hard tears are dripping on my steering wheel.

I search around my car to find a few tissues and I glance over at my dad and I'm shocked to find he's crying as hard as I am. "*Manari mou*, please forgive an old angry man."

"Oh, Dad —" I whisper.

"I should not be yelling at you, but it does no good to yell at God because he does not bring my son back. I cannot yell at your brother because he is already gone and even if I had known he was leaving, he wouldn't have listened to me. He always had wild ideas of his own and never consulted with me. I most certainly cannot yell at your mother because her heart breaks every morning when the sun rises again. She's crushed every time she opens her eyes and her baby no longer takes a breath on this planet. The person I yell at the most is me."

My heart is breaking over my dad's pain. I have never heard some of this.

My dad continues as if a dam has broken. "Why did I not know something was wrong with my son? He was the spitting image of me down to his wandering artist's soul. How could I not see through his ruse? Why did I believe him when he told me things were fine? I should've known better. I should've known he wasn't strong enough to be away from his family. Why did I let him go away to college? He could've gone to college here. He could've painted his pictures anywhere. A good father keeps his family together to stay strong. Why did I let him talk me into letting him go to school so far away? If only I hadn't, he would still be here and you would not be leaving me too."

"Daddy, I was always going to grow up and figure out my own way in life regardless of what happened with Onyx. I couldn't stay your little lamb forever. Onyx and I made these plans years ago. I was probably in junior high when we first talked about the possibility that I might not want to grow up to be a tattoo artist."

My dad looks completely befuddled. "Really? Why is this the first time I have heard of this?"

"Daddy, I know how much Ink'd Deep means to you. It's always been like your first child. I never wanted to let you down. I thought I'd wait until Ink'd Deep was safely in Onyx's hands and then I would go to school to become a teacher," I confess in a rush of speech.

I cautiously peek over at my dad to gauge his reaction to my announcement. I'm surprised when I see a slightly soggy look of amazement on his face.

"What?" I ask defensively.

He smirks at me. "You realize you just told me you want to be a teacher with about the same amount of wind up and delivery as most girls use to tell their parents they plan to move to Nevada to work for a brothel."

"To be honest, I thought I might get more support if I told you I was running away to Vegas."

My dad rubs his beard. "I can't argue with your point there. I've never been one for the traditional life — that's more your mother's thing. She'll be thrilled. There's nothing more perfect than a teacher and a librarian in the same family. I have to tell you I'm not excited about you going away to college. Seeing as it didn't work out so well for us the last time. Do you have to go away to college? Can't you take college classes around here? Can you go to college part-time? Will you still work at the shop? I don't want you to leave. Do you hate this life so bad you need to leave?"

The man who has been larger than life and my protector from the moment I took my first breath on this planet, looks so defeated I hardly recognize him. I haven't seen him look this sad since the day we buried Onyx. I try to climb over the console in my car to cuddle with my dad. At this point, the fact that I'm an adult seems immaterial. I need my dad and my dad needs me. I get as close as I can and hug him as I try to explain, "Dad, I swear — it's not about turning my back on Ink'd Deep. It's about trying to find out who I'm supposed to be. I never had a chance to figure it out on my own. Someone has always had expectations of what I was supposed to be and most of those expectations had something to do with Ink'd Deep. I want to separate myself from the shop and see if I can shine on my own."

I feel my dad's arms come around me and hug me tight. "Jade, you are the daughter of Diamond Petros. Of course you will shine like the brightest star regardless of what you choose to do. You are perfect, like your mother."

I sigh and kiss my father on the cheek. I can't resist one last comment, "Daddy, if I'm so perfect, why do you insist on treating me as if I am a dense apprentice who doesn't know the difference between a light switch and a lightning bug?"

'I don't know, *Manari mou*, perhaps you are not the only one who needs a vacation."

I'm busy trying to repair the ravages of my makeup in the break room and stuff a few bites of junk food in my mouth when Rogue comes in to fill her coffee cup. Rogue is one of those people I find intimidating. She doesn't try to be intimidating; it comes naturally. She is always effortlessly put together; she can take a plain white T-shirt, a pair of jeans and an old pair of tennis shoes and make them look like a fashion statement without any effort at all. For some reason, when I try the same look, I look like a juvenile delinquent. When she stops dead in her tracks after she catches a glimpse of me, it doesn't do wonders for my ego, let's put it that way.

"What happened to you? I thought you and Jett went out to lunch. What did you do, get robbed?" She studies me for clues.

I shrug. "No, we had a very emotional conversation because I was a little more honest than usual. I took a risk and told my dad I want to go to school like Onyx. He didn't know I have always planned to be a teacher."

Rogue's mouth rounds with surprise, but then she comments, "It might be a little bumpy at first, but I bet Jett will be a lot like Ivy's dad, Robert, and he'll come around without too much trouble — remember when she told him she wanted to change her major from accounting to art?"

"That's right, I had forgotten about that. He eventually was all right with the decision, right?"

"Almost instantaneously — I think Ivy was more worried about it than Robert was. I'd like to talk to you more about it, but you have an appointment coming in. Didn't you check your calendar?"

"Geez, I forgot to sync my calendar this morning. What did I miss?" I ask, flipping through my phone.

"As far as I can tell, these look like repeat customers for you — Allie and Ashley ring a bell?"

I almost choke on my Doritos when she mentions the names. "Seriously? I didn't expect them back quite so quickly." I stand up and go over to my portable drawing portfolio and remove several sketches I'd worked on from home. Ashley Nicole's drawing was one I had been puzzling out in my head for a while. The time I was home with Declan gave me some freedom to sketch several designs. I even had time to color them in with colored pencils. That's not a luxury I get here at the shop very often.

I try one more time to straighten my wild hair and I put on some lip gloss as I try to affect some sort of game face. I am a little surprised when I enter the shop floor and see Ashley and Allie with a tall, dark-haired guy. He doesn't look old enough to be their father, but he is dressed in a suit.

I greet the girls with a smile, "Hey! How are you? I've got some great stuff to show you." I turn to the gentleman accompanying them and hold out my hand for him to shake, but before I can say anything, Allie bursts into the conversation, "Jade, this is Mark, he was the one I was telling you about … you know, Callum's brother.

After we went home the other day, I got to thinking about what you said about family. I realized Callum would've been proud of what he did and what all of those drawings stood for. He would've wanted me to be proud of us too and he wouldn't want me to keep the drawings to myself. So, I reached out to his brother. Mark has a few questions for you. I hope you don't mind I brought him along."

Having lost my own brother, I feel an instant connection with the pain in Mark's eyes. I shake his hand. "Welcome to Ink'd Deep. I'm Jade. I'm sorry for your loss. It's a special kind of pain to be the sibling left behind."

"Ah, so Allie is correct; you are a kindred spirit in grief. It saddens me that you are touched by sorrow too," he comments somberly.

I shrug as I draw in a shaky breath. Today has been a flippin' emotional roller coaster. "Some days are worse than others, for sure. Allie mentioned you had questions. What can I do for you?"

Mark runs his hand through his short-cropped jet-black hair as he blows out a deep breath. "Here's the thing, I don't know how to say this without sounding like a complete jerk. Allie here tells me you're some hotshot television star and I should respect your talent as a tattoo artist. I see the type of people who are on television these days. It doesn't seem like it takes much talent at all to get your own cable show. I have no idea if you can even draw. My standards are high. My brother was an exceptional artist. Very few people knew how good he was, I'm not even sure he knew how good he was. If someone is going to be interpreting my brother's work and slapping it on somebody's skin where it'll last forever, I want to make damn sure they know what they're doing. I don't want somebody making a mockery of my brother's work."

I raise my eyebrow and cross my arms as I listen to his monologue. When he finishes, I nod and walk over to my portfolio book and open it. "It so happens I completely agree with you. I wouldn't want just any tattoo artist to do my work either. You should always choose very carefully." I walk over to Allie and look her directly in the eye as I instruct, "Allie, if at any time you feel like I'm not the artist for you, that's totally okay. I want you to be happy with who you choose."

She flushes bright red. "No worries. This isn't about me. I'm totally stoked. I just needed to show Mark what you're all about. He doesn't know who you are. Do you have time to do me today?"

I glance up at the clock and back at the file with Allie's design. Tapping the end of the pencil on my bottom lip in indecision, I finally concede, "I can't do both tattoos today. I could get the outline of your tattoo done today, but there is no way I can color it today."

"I read somewhere it's better to do the outlines first anyway," Allie responds.

"Everybody's skin reacts differently to the ink and everyone has a different tolerance, so it's hard to make a generalization. There are a lot of fine lines in Callum's design. They can take a toll on a tattoo artist, even an experienced one. A lot of times it's better to take a complex design in multiple stages."

"Are you working on the eleventh?" Allie asks me in a voice barely above a whisper.

I nod. "Yes, as far as I know."

Allie's spine straightens and she announces in a

steadier voice, "I know what I want you to do. I want you to do the outline today, but finish it on the eleventh. That's the second anniversary of the first time Callum asked me to marry him. It's a very special day for me and I want another happy memory to look back on when I remember that day."

Without conscious thought, I look over to the couches where Mark is studying the portfolios. I know technically Allie does not need his approval to get the tattoo, but I always breathe a little sigh of relief if everyone is on the same page. I'm not sure what he's looking at, but his face is a cauldron of emotion. I touch Allie on the shoulder as I pass her. "Excuse me, I need to see what's going on."

It all makes sense when I see the picture of the tattoo he is gently tracing with his finger. It was probably one of the hardest tattoos I've ever had to do. Those kind always are. He looks up at me with a haunted expression on his face. "How did you get this picture? She looks just like my daughter, Ketki. You and I have *never* met." He turns toward Allie and asks, "Did you and Callum show her a photograph?"

Allie vigorously shakes her head no as she replies, "No! Barbara Ann, Ashley Nicole and I came in here to celebrate surviving our first set of college exams. I thought I recognized this place from *Over It* but, never in a million years did I think Jade would be the one tattooing us."

Mark pins me with a narrowed gaze. "Then how do you explain it?"

"Do you mind?" I reach for the portfolio book. He hands it over and I gently extract a picture from behind the picture of the tattoo.

"This is the little girl I tattooed on her daddy. He sent his wife and daughter on a plane on September 11th to go visit his parents. They were planning on touring the East Coast and visiting the White House after he wrapped up some contract negotiations with his business. They never made it because their plane crashed into the World Trade Center. As far as I know, she has nothing to do with your family — but it is one of the most beautiful portraits I've ever done."

Mark's hands are shaking as he pulls his wallet out from his back pocket and removes a picture. The little girl in the picture is a little younger than the reference picture I used for the tattoo, but they could have easily been the same child. It's enough to send a chill up my spine. "Wow, that's uncanny."

Mark takes a swig of water from his water bottle and wipes his eyes before continuing, "I don't know, perhaps the saddest coincidence of all are the horrendous acts of terrorists which tie our stories together. Maybe that was Callum's point all along." He walks over to Allie and collects her into an embrace. After a while, he pulls away and cups her cheek. "I don't know who my brother thought he was fooling. He wasn't keeping you a secret from anyone. We all knew he had given you his heart on the first day you met. He was waiting for you to grow up. If anyone should wear his artwork, it's you. Jade should do it because I think Callum chose her."

CHAPTER EIGHT

DECLAN

I MIGHT HAVE TO admit I could easily become addicted to all of Jade's gadgets. I live a minimalist lifestyle since I generally take most of my stuff with me on the road. I learned a long time ago it's not safe to leave anything of value behind. Typically, I don't keep a lot of gadgets around; even my cell phone is a few models behind the current trend. It's functional and it works — which is all I usually need. However, being banged up has added some new items to my wish list.

When I mentioned I wanted to write music again, Jade came up with an ingenious solution. She let me borrow her iPad. I haven't had a chance to play around with a tablet for several years and the last time I used one they didn't do much. But she has a program on this thing which allows me to play instruments with a stylus and record my voice. I discovered I can jam the stylus between my cast and my fingers, so I can almost play this thing two-handed. It's cool because there's a piano on the little tablet. For an electronic device, it plays decently. It's been helpful in songwriting. At least it's giving me something to do while I lie around.

I received more good news today. One of my

musician friends is using one of my songs on his album. He cut me a royalty check for the rights to the song and I celebrated by calling my friend who is a waitress at Frannie's to order some takeout. Rogue offered to bring it by because Jade is staying late to work on a couple of customers tonight. I thought it would be cool to surprise her because she's been at my beck and call for days. As much as there's a part of me which enjoys being spoiled, it's a little embarrassing not to be able to reciprocate.

After I finish setting up the coffee table for our dinner for two, I settle back into songwriting mode. I'm playing the little piano instead of the guitar and talking into the recorder on the iPad instead of writing. It's a different way to compose, but it's better than nothing. The only downside is it takes about ten times as long to do it this way. There's something about processing my words through handwriting that's missing with this method. I don't seem to remember what I've composed as well and I keep having to go back and rewind my lyrics to make sure everything is cohesive. I'm so engrossed in what I'm doing, I don't even hear the back door open until someone is standing in the kitchen.

I look up, fully expecting it to be Rogue. I'm startled to find Jade standing in front of me. Much to my horror, Jade looks as if someone or something has completely unraveled her soul. Physically, she looks relatively unchanged from this morning — except her eyes are red and puffy and she looks exhausted. However, her eyes are filled with unfathomable pain. This is a pain beyond her stiff neck or sore shoulder, this comes from questioning who you are and why you exist and not being fully satisfied with the answers you come up with.

Without a word, I put the iPad down and walk over

to her and gather her up into an embrace as I try to siphon her pain away. We stand there silently for several minutes because I know with pain like this, words feel like sandpaper. Eventually, Jade pulls away, wiping her eyes on her sweatshirt sleeves. I pull her close for one more moment as I place a soft kiss on her forehead and whisper, "I'm sorry you hurt, J."

Jade walks over to the counter, grabs a paper towel, wipes her face and blows her nose. She grabs a soda from the fridge and fiddles with the can. She doesn't even try to open it. She needs something in her hands as she unloads about her day.

"Today was tough," she states matter-of-factly.

I walk over to her, place my arm around her waist and escort her to the couch. Tucking her next to me, I encourage her to continue, "I kind of figured that out. What happened?"

"Part of it was my own stupidity, I don't know what I was expecting. Marcus has never been a big fan of paperwork and I don't know why I expected him to change. When I got back to the shop, my desk was completely buried in crap; it's like my dad and Marcus did nothing the whole time I've been gone. Rogue tried to keep it up, but it's not her job. She's an apprentice and there are certain things she can't do yet. She was the one who noticed we have a supplier who keeps shorting us on our ink orders. I was in the middle of trying to straighten all that out and figure out how many months it's been happening when my dad came in and started giving me a hard time for taking time off."

"I'm sorry, J. I didn't mean to cause problems between you." I hug her closer.

"It's okay. It wasn't you. This has been a long time coming. Today was just the last straw. I don't know if you've noticed, but I take the least amount of time off of anybody in the whole business. I'm not complaining. I haven't had much else to do with my life. I'm not like Rogue where I'm trying to balance school quite as much. The online classes I take don't take nearly as much time as her studio classes. I don't do nearly as much volunteering as Marcus and Tristan." Her lip hitches up in a funny grin. "Then again, I don't have a private plane either."

"J, I'm confused," I interject. "Are you apologizing because you're stressed out? In case you haven't noticed, things have been chaotic recently and some crappy stuff has happened in the world lately."

She collapses a little against my shoulder as she wipes her eyes with the paper towel. "No, it's more complicated than that. I'm apologizing because I completely got up in my dad's face today and I feel bad about it, but what I said to him wasn't wrong. I'm sorry because it hurt him. I never, ever wanted to do that. He was crushed. Today was the first time we had an honest conversation about how angry he was that Onyx committed suicide. It broke my heart that we had to talk about it in the parking lot. My car needed to be cleaned out weeks ago because there was a bunch of garbage all over it. It wasn't the place to have life-changing discussions. It was too sad," she admits. "I never ever wanted it to go down that way. I had a whole strategy I planned to follow. My good intentions were blown out of the water when he chewed me out for taking care of you."

I kiss the top of her head. "Jade, I've known your dad for a long time and I know he often runs his mouth before he engages his brain. He's a good guy, but he often forgets to show that side of himself. He can let go on one of his tirades and forget someone else is in the room, let alone consider he might hurt someone else's feelings. The bottom line is there's no excuse for him to lash out at you. I'm sorry he was mean to you."

"It wasn't all his fault. I've been swallowing my feelings for a long time. This conversation was bound to happen sooner or later. We had lots of things to say to each other, but I regret the timing. It shouldn't have happened in the middle of the workday. It was way too much emotion to handle at work. It started being about vacation and ended up being about why Onyx committed suicide. It was unreal."

"I'm sorry Jade, I wish I'd been there for you, that's a lot to handle on any day."

"You don't even know the half of it," Jade remarks, drilling the heels of her hands into her temples in small circles, as if to wipe away fatigue. "Remember the other day when we went out to lunch after my clients left?"

I nod. "I figured they would probably be back. It was only your dad who was having a conniption fit. I know how you operate. You don't want to do any work on someone unless you're absolutely certain they are sure about the plan. I wish I would've had a tattoo artist like you for my first few tattoos; if I had, you would be doing a lot less cover up work on me," I remark with an embarrassed grimace.

"One of them was a memorial tattoo of sorts, her boyfriend was killed in one of the terrorist bombings in France. He was an artist who was innocently attending a concert."

"Do you have some psychic gift which draws these people to you or something? Isn't this like the third memorial tattoo you've done involving a victim of a terrorist attack?"

"The actual number is much higher. I don't talk about it much. I even did a small piece on a young woman who lost a family member on an airplane in the Ukraine. I will never know how she found me in the middle of Florida."

"You're amazing," I murmur.

Jade shrugs. "The tattoo today was sad on so many levels. Allie and Callum were so young and fell in love at first sight. Callum had already escaped one terrorist attack only to be taken down by another. I met his brother, Mark, who has his own tragic tale but had to bury his little brother too. I felt so bad for him, he came face-to-face with one of the other memorial tattoos I had done from yet another victim of a mass tragedy — domestic terrorism, they call it these days — and it was like he had seen the ghost of his own child. After he showed me a picture of his daughter, I totally understand why — the kids could have been identical twins. They look about as much alike as Ivy and Rogue. It was enough to make the hair on the back of my neck stand up. You know I'm used to creepy stuff I can't explain with the spooky twins, but this was above and beyond. Mark was shaken by the whole experience. In the end, he was perfectly fine with his brother's fiancée getting a tattoo of the drawing his little brother created. At least the part where I gave her ink ended up being successful."

"Why do you still look so devastated? It sounds like things are working okay with your dad," I ask, still concerned about her closed off body language and her look of total fatigue.

"I don't know. I think I may have worked out a temporary truce with Dad as long as I can balance school and staying a part of the family biz. He doesn't want me to leave the business entirely. Honestly though, I'm not sure how I'm going to handle it all, especially after an emotional day like today. Today's tattoos took it out of me mentally."

"Were those the tattoos you were working on this weekend?" I ask, remembering the symbolic design.

"Yes, she settled on the small watercolor butterfly with the semi colon, but she had it placed on her inner wrist, which is a tender spot to tattoo and it was a difficult topic for both of us. She talked about her guilt over not knowing her friend needed her help. I wanted to listen to her story, I really did. It was like reliving all the conversations I had in my head after Onyx killed himself."

"I'm so sorry, J," I whisper against her temple.

"It was excruciatingly hard to provide emotional support for her when I don't feel like I have the answers. Sometimes, I wonder if I should go to school to be a teacher or if I'd be better suited as a mental health counselor. I'm probably a natural at counseling. I've been unofficially doing it for years."

"True enough."

"Being a tattoo artist is harder than it looks. People tell you their most intimate stories even if you don't feel capable of dealing with them. I suppose she felt like she could trust me with her feelings because she knew about Onyx. After my emotional confrontation with my dad, it was the last thing I wanted to deal with today. I didn't even know they were coming in today or I would have been more prepared, I guess. The whole thing kind of threw me for a loop."

I reach over and fluff the pillow behind her. "I've got things handled tonight, so put your feet up and relax. Try to set it aside for a few hours." Finally, she seems to stop and take a moment to look around.

Impulsively, she throws her arms around my neck and kisses me as she says, "This is so sweet! But … um … where's the food?"

I gently extract her arms from my neck as I try not to grimace in pain. "For some reason, you beat Rogue here. That wasn't exactly the plan."

Jade looks sheepish for a moment and then she remarks, "I'm sorry, we had a walk-in and I assigned him to Rogue. I didn't know you two were co-conspirators."

"That was kind of the point. It couldn't be a surprise if I told you about it. I didn't know about it until the last minute either. But I figured I don't get news like this very often so I might as well celebrate."

Jade raises an eyebrow at me as she remarks, "After the month you've had, you could use some good news. Go ahead, lay it on me. I need a mood adjustment today."

"You remember my friend, Joe Summers? I brought him in a couple years ago because he needed a tattoo cover-up."

Jade concentrates for a couple moments and then answers, "Isn't he the guy who had his girlfriend's initials on his shoulder?"

"That's him," I confirm.

"I offered him a few cover-up designs, but he didn't

seem ready—"

I shake my head in dismay. "He needed to be ready a while ago. Unfortunately, he seems to be the last one to figure it out. Anyway, he teaches music therapy to kids with autism. He made a demo tape and apparently some producer somewhere saw it. The studio head wants him to make a demo tape for his record label. Since Joe's using a song I wrote for him, he cut me an advance royalty check. Tonight we're having a celebration dinner."

"That's so cool! You can be one of those people who says, 'I knew Joe back before he could even carry a tune,'" Jade replies with a wide grin. "Seriously though, what a stand-up guy to pay it forward before he even knows if it'll be a sure thing."

"It was," I concede.

"I met a pretty cool guy today too. He was the brother of the guy I was memorializing. At first, he was all kinds of skeptical. In the end, he made his own appointment for a back piece. It takes a real gentleman to do such an epic one-eighty with so much grace. I offered to do his tat for free too because of his brother, but he turned me down and said I deserved to be paid for my work."

I can't help but smirk. "That ought to make Jett happy. You booked an extra client off the whole deal."

Jade chokes back a bark of laughter. "I know, right? I think Dad forgets Ink'd Deep is a booming, successful business. He still treats it like the early days when he had a couple of chairs above Grandpa Petros' boat shop. Every time he's upset with me, he pulls out the old photo albums and reminisces about how he built the business from the ground up and how children aren't appropriately grateful for what their parents do for them."

"I don't see that in you at all. You've stuck by your parents during the hardest of times — which is way more than I've done for mine. When times got tough in my family, I split."

Jade starts to respond but we are interrupted by a knock at the door. She moves to get up but I pull her back down onto the couch as I chide, "Remember, I've got this."

"If I know Rogue, she got enough food to feed half the population of Gainesville. You'll need another set of hands," she warns.

I shrug. "Whatever. Let's not leave her standing out there, I'm starving."

As soon as I open the front door, Rogue points her index finger at Jade's chest as she states, "You don't even know how much you owe me. Did you ever talk to this guy? Who in the world walks into a tattoo salon with absolutely no idea what they want? This guy was all over the map. One minute he wanted Dory from *Finding Nemo*, the next minute he wanted *Dexter*. I'm so glad Marcus was there working on the Jameson twins, otherwise I would've been fully creeped out."

"What did he finally choose?" I asked, curiosity getting the best of me.

"That was the bizarre thing — we never even got that far in our very long consultation. Suddenly he got all up in arms about me being able to certify the conditions under which my ink is manufactured. I can only go by what it says on the bottle. I can't personally testify to how the company manufactures its tattoo ink. He stormed out of the shop blustering about how we support child labor and indentured servitude. I'm sorry, Jade, I may have bought us another negative review. I swear I didn't do anything to this guy. I was trying to work with him."

Jade puts one arm around Rogue's shoulder and picks up a bag of food with the other. "Seriously, don't worry about it. He sounds like the type of person who would've given the shop a bad review regardless of what you did. Remember the person who liked their tattoo a lot, but did not like the kind of magazines we had in the waiting room?"

Rogue nods. "I forgot about that. You're right, people are a little nuts. Pounding on some nails with my husband at the Habitat for Humanity house should make me feel better."

"Isn't it a little dark outside?"

"That's what floodlights are for. You'd be surprised by how fast we put those houses up because we can work nearly round-the-clock."

I walk over to Rogue and shake her hand. "Thank you so much, I owe you one."

"No problem, Gimpy. Be sure to treat my boss-lady right. She's one in a million," Rogue advises, as she says her goodbyes to Jade and heads out the door with a wink.

CHAPTER NINE

JADE

IT'S WEIRD. WHEN ONYX died, it's almost as if part of my identity died as well. I lost part of who I am and what my plans were for the future. As a little girl, I always figured we would have a big family with lots of nieces and nephews running around. With Onyx gone that dream died too. I stopped being someone's little sister. For the first time in my life, I'm an only child. I don't know what my definition of family is anymore. It's not what I thought it was before. I didn't realize what a solitary existence I was leading, despite the very social nature of my job, until Declan moved into my house.

House. What a very funny descriptive word. Technically, that's what I have. For the most part, it's boring and average. My dad helped me put in the garden tub in the bathroom, but beyond that, it's typical. The important thing to me is it's mine. I was proud of the fact I was able to buy it a few weeks shy of my twenty-first birthday — not very many people my age can say that. Although it's mine, it's never truly felt like a home until I had someone to share it with.

Declan has been hysterical comic relief, in ways I never expected. One morning I was teasing him about not refilling the toilet paper roll in the bathroom and always hanging the toilet paper backwards. When I came back from work, there was a freestanding toilet paper holder and Declan had added a sign which read, "MINE. Problem Solved." Of course, he hung the toilet paper totally backwards. I helpfully fixed it for him. Thus began the TP Wars. He in turn, fixed mine. Obviously, I had to do better. So, I bought him a roll of specialty toilet paper with crossword puzzles on it. Somewhere, he found me toilet paper designed for women going through divorce. It had all sorts of men's names on it and hung it on my toilet paper holder. I got him some with the word poop written in several languages. He declared the roll a collector's item and wouldn't put it on his toilet paper dispenser, so we are at a temporary impasse. Every time I think about our silly little game, it makes me smile. In fact, a lot of things about Declan make me smile. He claims he doesn't like cats, but he sleeps with Inkblot every day. He even made him a homemade cat bed out of an old concert T-shirt and I routinely catch him giving him bites of table scraps.

For a man who doesn't like putting down roots, he has turned my average little house into a real home. I'm not even sure how to explain how having Declan's company has changed me. Even though we often fight like an old married couple, his presence has reminded me what I was like before Onyx died. I feel more authentic around him. It's as if I don't have to put on my social body armor. I can be Jade Crystal Petros, the slightly odd woman who doesn't quite fit anywhere. Declan doesn't seem to be put off by my eccentricities.

I didn't set out to find myself a partner. Although it's been amusing to watch my friends fall in love like timber at a logging competition, I never figured it would happen to me. All of a sudden, as I think about the future, Declan is in the picture with me. I'm reluctant to even admit it to myself. Declan is everything I want to turn away from, his lifestyle is completely opposite of the one I want to pursue. My whole life has been all about following your bliss and doing whatever your artistic muse directs. Most kids want to run away and join the circus, my parents *were* the circus. Even though my mom is a librarian, she was remarkably casual about education. She always felt I could learn whatever I needed to learn through reading on my own. Fortunately for me, I had a teacher in the seventh grade who reached out and gave me the love of learning. I want to be that kind of teacher for some other kid who doesn't quite fit in to social norms. All of this brings me back to Declan. I simply don't know what to do with the man. I never expected to like him as much as I do. He pushes my buttons in all the best ways.

I wish Onyx was here to tell me what to do. He could always cut to the heart of the matter with a few well-chosen words. I try to imagine what he might say about my current predicament. I remember the last time I was with Onyx and my grandmother. We were making homemade ice cream in an old-fashioned ice cream maker you had to hand-crank. Onyx was complaining about his girlfriend's taste in music and my grandmother told him the universe would provide us with who we needed but not necessarily who we wanted. It was our responsibility to decide to get along. I always thought it was funny advice for my grandmother to give because she and grandpa fought like cats and dogs.

If Onyx were here, I expect he would tell me I need to suck it up and decide what's most important to me. Although it's tempting to be cautious and play it safe, I know my heart is telling me something very different.

Declan snaps his fingers in front of my face. "I know it's been a long day, but did you fall asleep sitting up?"

I shake my head as I respond, "No, I'm thinking."

He opens a little cardboard container and shows it to me as he asks, "Do you want this warmed up?"

"You got bread pudding for dessert? I thought you hated raisins."

He shrugs as he answers, "I do, but I can pick them out of my part. I know you like this, so I got it for you."

I take the box out of his hand and set it back down on the coffee table. "For a guy who likes to project the image that you don't care about much, you definitely pay attention to the small details. I appreciate it," I remark as I bury my hands in his hair and pull him closer for a kiss. I've spent an embarrassingly large amount of time imagining what this would feel like over the past months since he admitted in the hospital he wanted to kiss me. Even so, my fantasies couldn't match the reality. I feel myself melt into him as I knead the back of his head and take the kiss deeper.

Declan pulls away and then rests his forehead against mine as he struggles to catch his breath. He groans softly. "I hope that kiss means what I hope it means, because I'd hate to misunderstand at this point." He leans in to kiss me again. "I take it this has a little something to do with what you were thinking about?"

I nod. "It does. I threw caution to the wind and followed my heart and sent my worries on vacation."

Declan pulls away from me and unthreads my hands from his neck. "I'm not sure I like the sound of that. I don't want to be anybody's regret."

I cringe at his response. "I'm sorry, I didn't mean it

like that. I didn't expect to have you or anyone else in my life right now. I've got a lot of crazy stuff going on unrelated to you. At first, I thought I could keep my relationship with you separate from all the rest of the chaos going on in my life, but it's become apparent that's not possible. Having you in my life has changed the way I approach my life. Knowing you are here supporting me makes me stronger, bolder and truer to myself — my life will probably become a lot more complicated soon."

"Jade, I'm sorry; I must be dense here, but it sounds like those are good things, right?" Declan asks, his confusion clear on his face.

I feel like I'm a fish out of water as I flail around trying to explain my chaotic mental gymnastics.

"Look, I don't know if I can explain all this to you, but you may have noticed I don't have a lot of boyfriends — despite all the chronic couple-ness that's spread like a virus at Ink'd Deep."

"Trust me, I've noticed," Declan responds with a sheepish grin. "Is it wrong of me to admit I cheer every time you go on a date and don't end up with the guy?"

I try to muster up an appropriate amount of offense; but I guess if I'm honest with myself, I'm relieved he hasn't hooked up with some random groupie too — but then again maybe he has and just hasn't brought her around the shop.

"Come on J, you can't clam up on me now. I can't begin to guess where you are going with this," Declan cajoles.

"I suppose you think it's because I can't get a date?" I challenge.

"No!" Declan protests. "A person would be crazy to

think that. If anything, people might be a little intimidated by Jett. Your dad is scary when he wants to be. Anybody else might assume you already have somebody. You are too drop-dead gorgeous to be single."

Jade sighs. "It always comes down to that, doesn't it? People can't seem to get past what I look like and bother to figure out who I am as a person. It only got worse after Onyx died and I started to get famous in tattoo circles. After *Over It* gained popularity in the ratings, reporters and paparazzi tried to go out with me to see if they could dig up any dirt. At first, I was naïve enough to believe they were interested in me. As the old cliché goes, I believed my own press. As the stories about me got wilder, so did I. There was a time after Onyx died when I almost didn't care what people thought of me. I lost my internal compass for a bit. I became whoever the tabloids wanted me to be. I'm not that person — but somehow I believed it was good for business for me to be edgy, wild and impulsive. The more I became that person, the more uncomfortable I became. I stopped socializing altogether and threw myself into work. I seem to have a hard time balancing who I am with who people expect me to be. I have this reputation for being hard and emotionless — people think I don't care about what other people think. The reality is I care far too much."

Declan nods slowly. "I think I get it now." He pulls away from me and walks toward the front door. He grabs his lyric notebook off the kitchen table as he mutters, "J, you had me all kinds of fooled. I thought we were different."

I'm watching this unfold in front of me with a sense of bizarre detachment. It isn't until his hand is on the door handle that I come crashing back to reality and blurt, "Wait! What are you doing?"

Declan turns back toward me with a savage expression on his face as he sneers, "What does it look like I'm doing? I'm leaving; you made it clear enough. I don't have to be asked twice."

"What are you talking about?" I ask incredulously. "You weren't even asked once. Wasn't I climbing your body a few minutes ago? I definitely want you here."

"So I'm good enough to warm your bed, but not be your boyfriend?" he asks sarcastically, "Of course, who would want to date a stupid street musician?"

Instinctively, I protest, "No, that's not what I'm saying. I'm not ashamed of you. I know how hard you work. Geez! Declan, get real. I'm a tattoo artist. Do I have room to judge anybody's career choices?"

"Then tell me what the heck you meant," Declan challenges.

I hug Inkblot close for comfort as I struggle to find the words. This conversation is part of the weird dichotomy of me that I've been trying to explain. I'm known for being upfront and bluntly honest with people — but there's a huge caveat. I'm also reluctant to cause chaos and pain. When being honest is likely to hurt someone's feelings, it's very hard for me to say anything, but I know Declan needs to know.

"Okay, so this is about your job — but, it's not in the way you think it is —" I start to explain.

Declan rolls his eyes as he responds, "This should be good. I can't wait to hear you talk your way out of this mess."

His flippant response pisses me off and I retort, "If you're not interested in what I have to say, you can keep heading out the door."

Declan stops in his tracks and turns around and flops down in the side chair next to the couch. "By all means, feel free to enlighten me."

Ignoring his goading tone, I continue, "Before you came into my life, I wasn't looking for anybody. After our conversation at the restaurant, I *really* wasn't looking for you. You stomped on my dreams and dismissed them as silly and unimportant. I don't need another voice like that in my life. Honestly, had fate not intervened, I'm not sure if we'd still be friends. I was completely disappointed in the way you mowed right over me. When you came to live with me, I was introduced to a whole other side of you — a side I like very much, by the way. I was left to figure out which Declan would show up if we were in a relationship. Would it be the one who would question my hopes and dreams or would it be the one who is nurturing and supporting?"

Declan leans forward and buries his face in his hands for a moment. When he finally straightens, his eyes are red and his jaw is tight. If I look carefully, I can still see yellow bruising around his jawline and eye socket. "The day I was attacked is fuzzy for me. But, I remember being confused about why you were upset with me. Now that I've spent time with you, I understand. I apologize for not understanding back then. I shouldn't have spouted off about stuff I didn't understand. From the outside looking in, your job looks like what I dream of having. You have financial security, artistic freedom and a team of family and coworkers who support and love you. If I were in your shoes, I couldn't imagine giving that up for the unknown," Declan explains.

"But you did," I counter. "How is my becoming a

teacher any different from you leaving your family's car business to become a musician?"

"It's not, I was being hardheaded. I felt like my artistic calling was somehow better than being a teacher and helping kids. I know — you don't have to judge me. I'm kicking myself for being such an idiot."

I study Declan carefully. He seems genuinely remorseful. It is true, we had a lot of preconceptions about each other before this unexpected social experiment threw us together — or perhaps as my grandmother believed, it's the universe giving us a chance to find each other. One more thought occurs to me. "After all we've been through together, why were you so quick to believe I was asking you to leave? Why would you believe I, of all people, would be ashamed of you?"

Declan flushes and stammers, "I don't have many people in my life who believe in what I do. Most people treat me like I'm an overgrown teenager who hasn't found myself yet. I guess I thought you'd be ashamed of me because most people are."

I get up from the couch and walk over to Declan's chair and kiss him gently on the lips. "I can't say I totally understand why you do what you do, but I'm trying. Does that count?"

Chapter Ten

Declan

THE WAIT IS ABSOLUTELY KILLING me, but I hope it's worth it. I can't believe I was able to score this treat for Jade. Sometimes, bartering has its advantages. All I had to do was agree to perform for two day cruises and this guy gave me an evening cruise in exchange. Hopefully, this will help make up for me being a total nimrod and almost ruining our relationship. Today she's doing a mastectomy cover-up tattoo. She's explained the unique challenge to me before. She never knows how long it will take because the scar tissue can react differently.

Jett walks by the break room table and catches me writing in the lyric notebook. "Your cast is off. My daughter doesn't need to be your nursemaid anymore. When are you taking off?"

"I'll be around for a while. I've got physical therapy. I have some residual damage. Those punks got me good with a knife," I remark with a nonchalant shrug.

"Maybe you should go into a safer line of work," Jett observes dryly.

"Says the guy who rides a motorcycle and goes skydiving," parries Jade as she walks over and kisses me soundly.

I almost fall out of my chair, I'm so shocked. I wasn't aware we had announced the change in our relationship status to our parents yet and this is a rather in-your-face way to go about it.

"Jade Crystal Petros, I thought you had better manners than to lie to your parents —" Jett bellows.

"Daddy, relax. This is the first time I've seen you all week and up until this week, Declan was merely my roommate. I didn't lie. What was I supposed to do, send you a text message when you and mom were on your anniversary trip?"

"Did you have to settle for a homeless drifter?" he asks.

Diamond Petros comes around the corner with a stack of books for me and nails her husband with a dark look as she says, "Peter Petros, I'm sure I must have misunderstood you because I'm positive you could not have said what I thought you said."

He looks back and forth between us defensively as he sputters, "What? It's true. As far as I can tell he doesn't have a discernible job. How will he support our daughter?"

Diamond's eyes widen as she responds, "In case you haven't noticed, our daughter is fully capable of supporting herself. You sound like my father. As I recall, I worked swing shift while I went to school so you could get your shop up and running. If it wasn't for the generosity of our families, we would've never made it. We would probably still be living in a rickety old walk-up apartment somewhere. No offense Jett, but back in the early days you were no prize catch yourself. If I didn't have loyal customers at the pancake house, we would've been much hungrier, trust me."

"Sir—" I begin, but Jade beats me to the punch.

"Daddy, Declan doesn't try to tell you how to do your job, don't tell him how to do his. You have no idea what goes into what he does. He's an incredible musician. His songs are hauntingly beautiful. His work is pure poetry. Not only that, he can cover virtually anyone else's stuff. Do you know how hard it is to know past and current music trends and know when it's appropriate to play what? He has to read the mood of the crowd and respond accordingly. He takes requests and plays songs from memory. He plays music for five-year-old kids and eighty-five-year-old adults alike as he plays in churches and in gay bars and everywhere in between. Do you know he plays for people confined to hospital beds? He doesn't charge anything and doesn't accept tips for those performances. Declan also sings at the VFW. He donates his time. Did you even know he does all those gigs?"

"It's true, he donates his time for the Young Readers Camp too," Diamond interjects.

While their impassioned defense of me is embarrassing, it's also one of the coolest things to happen to me in quite some time. I am so used to having to justify my very existence that it's humbling to have someone else assign value to what I do — especially with such fire and passion.

Jett narrows his gaze at me as he demands, "How do you expect to earn a living if you sing for free?"

Diamond lays her hand on her husband's shoulder as she remarks, "Honey, you are being unfair. You and Jade donate a fair amount of your work hours away too."

"Yeah, but we can afford to put roofs over our heads," Jett argues.

"So can I, when I choose to make it a huge priority, but right now I'm focused on other things," I respond firmly as an alarm rings on my phone. "Jade, we need to go or we'll be late. Mr. and Mrs. Petros, if you'll excuse me, I would like to take your lovely daughter on an evening cruise. She's had a long day and could use some pampering."

It feels strange not to be the one playing the music. However, the owner of the cruise line told me not to worry about it and enjoy myself. The band tonight is fairly decent. They're playing some light jazz music and Jade seems to be enjoying herself. Dinner was delicious, and the chef did me a solid and fixed some bread pudding made from croissants. He even left the raisins out of mine. I felt terrible after our disagreement the other night because Jade lost her appetite and didn't feel like eating dessert.

When Jade noticed our desserts differed from everyone else's, she started to tear up and mumble about how much I spoil her. I felt ridiculously accomplished because I pulled off one little surprise. Not for the first time recently, I wondered what it would be like to be able to do this kind of stuff every day just to elicit Jade's watery grin and trembling kiss of joy.

At the moment, we are staring out the big picture window at a big flotilla of boats with Christmas lights. I'm standing behind her as she sways in time with the music. As Jade leans closer to the window to get a better view, I whisper in her ear, "You know the only true way to experience this is out on the deck."

Jade spins around in my arms and looks at me with her mouth agape. "Do you realize this is the end of December? It's freezing out there!"

I have to hide my grin. "First of all, this is Florida, you all don't know the meaning of the word freezing. Secondly, we are officially a couple now. I'm sure of it, given what you did in front of your dad today. We can share our body heat and I have a big wool jacket on, see?" I respond, pulling my jacket open and wrapping it around her.

Jade leans into me and drops a kiss on my Adam's apple. The surge of desire coursing through me is intense. If it hadn't been for the chair rail I'm propped up against, my knees would have buckled right there in front of a dining room full of people. My breathing quickens as I draw in a breath. Jade is quick to pick up on my reaction. She grins slowly. "You're right, I forgot about the perks of having a hot, hunky boyfriend. Sorry about this afternoon, I probably should've given you a heads up. That display was a little payback. When I was about thirteen, I told Onyx I was planning to kiss my first boy. Onyx thought this was a momentous occasion which should be witnessed by the whole family — so he told my parents."

Jett is overprotective now, I can only imagine what he would have been like when Jade was a teenager. "That must've been a tad awkward."

Jade laughs. "You have absolutely no idea. Rod Thomas may never be the same. He didn't look at me again, even in high school."

I grimace. "What did your dad do to him?"

Jade blushes and shakes her head as she recalls, "It wasn't so much what he did, as much as what he threatened to do in front of him. My dad said if he was so intent on making out with me, my dad would show him how to make out with a woman correctly. I've never seen a guy move so fast in my life. Rod was up and off my couch, his tennis shoes left streaks of rubber on my parents' carpet. It was too bad too, I had a rather large crush on him. Onyx knew — the whole situation was incredibly funny to my big brother."

"You waited all these years to pay your parents back? I'm a little scared," I joke.

"No, I'm not really bent on revenge. Since the perfect opportunity presented itself, I couldn't resist needling my dad a little. I hope you don't mind."

I hug her a little closer. "I guess it depends on how long your dad stays mad at me."

"I think he's well on his way toward forgiving you. I saw a thumbs-up as we were headed out the door. I think you won a few brownie points by taking me on a dinner cruise. This is nice; I've never done one of these before. I was a little afraid I might be seasick."

"You haven't seen anything until you've gone out on the deck," I grab Jade's hand and pull her toward the exit.

She laughs. "I still think you're crazy, do you see how I'm dressed? I am wearing a dress and high heels."

I wrap my coat around her and murmur in her ear, "What's the matter? Don't you trust me to keep you safe?"

Jade leans back against me. "I don't know — I trust you more than I've trusted anyone in years and maybe that's what scares me the most."

Her stark honesty makes me smile. I often feel the same way about our relationship. Many times, it feels like the exhilaration I get from bungee jumping. Sometimes, we have the pure excitement of a free-fall, only to be stopped short when we reach the bottom and start over again. It's an exciting ride, no matter how you look at it.

As I open the door to go out onto the deck, a large gust of cold wind hits us and her dress billows. She turns around. "Is it too late to change my mind?"

After we walk toward the railing, I rearrange my coat so it covers both of us. "Better?" I capture her hands between mine to warm them.

"Maybe… but I think my lips are still cold," she teases.

I let go of her hands and cup the back of her head as I kiss her deeply. I feel a bit like the star of a romantic drama as the wind whips our hair around. I remember seeing the movie *Titanic* in my English class and snickering with my friends in the back row, but I'm beginning to see the appeal as Jade snuggles close and clutches my waist.

I'm lost in the moment so I take a second to process what Jade's saying when she pulls away. "Not to be a mood killer here, but something is vibrating, and I don't think it's you."

Whatever she's saying isn't registering with me, so Jade pulls open my jacket and removes my phone and hands it to me. I shake my head and put it back in the pocket and resume kissing her. She grins up at me as she remarks, "I like a gentleman who has his priorities straight."

I hear an odd message tone — one I haven't heard in three years. I sway a bit on my feet.

Jade looks at me with alarm. "Seasick?"

I shake my head in response as I answer hoarsely, "J, I'm sorry I have to go inside and take this. I think it's my brother."

Jade takes me by the hand and opens the door to the lounge near the bar area. Almost quicker than I can get my phone out of my pocket and return Finn's phone call, she's back with a cup of coffee, sugar and cream. I don't know what's happening, but my calls aren't going through. Jade stands beside me and pulls my hair out of my face and removes my cell phone from my shaking hands. She looks at my call history and selects the phone number and pushes redial as she hands the phone back and whispers, "Breathe. It'll be okay."

Her quiet strength allows me to catch my breath as I hear the phone ring twice before Finn picks up.

His instructions are brief, "Better get home."

I feel like somebody is twisting a knife in my side as I ask, "Dad?"

"He's in recovery from a quadruple bypass as we speak. We're waiting to go see him."

"I thought he had a stent," I utter the first thing which comes to mind.

"Obviously it wasn't enough and you would know that if you'd bothered to stick around."

"I'll be there.

"I hope you're not too late," Finn replies gruffly.

His words are like physical blows to my psyche and I flinch. Jade has to catch my phone as it slips from my shoulder. As the blood rushes in my ears, I vaguely figure out she's speaking to Finn. I can see her nodding her head. She removes the pen from the drink tray and writes on the back of the receipt. Bizarrely, she hangs my phone up and puts it back in my pocket. She removes my credit card from the table and puts it back in my other pocket. Jade walks over and shrugs my jacket off of her shoulders and places it over mine and asks, "Ready to go back to our table?"

Numbly, I stand up and mumble a reply, "Yes. *No.* Oh, heck — I don't know. This is not how I thought tonight would go. I'm so sorry."

Jade runs her hand along the sleeve of my jacket as she says, "Look, if anybody knows anything about real life interrupting the life you imagined, it's me. Don't worry about it. Let's just worry about what is. We'll worry about what we hoped for later, okay?"

"J, I don't even know how I'll get to Jacksonville. My car doesn't run well enough to make it there. I have radiator problems. It will take too long on the bus. What if I don't make it there in time and my dad dies? We have too many things left unsaid between us. I don't know why I let it go on so long. Pride, I guess. I always thought he would be around forever. I'm such a stupid idiot. I knew he had issues because he has a stent, but he said it was *fine*. Mom said he was fine. It was all supposed to be fine. Why *isn't* it fine?" I ask, knowing there is no good answer.

CHAPTER ELEVEN

JADE

I HAVEN'T HAD A flood of adrenaline this large since the day we found my brother. Honestly, it's making me a bit nauseous. I have to keep it together because Declan seems lost in himself at the moment. It seemed like it took us forever to reach land. In reality, it was only about three hours, yet it seemed like three days. A dinner cruise is not the ideal place to get an emergency phone call from your family. By the time we are unloaded from the boat, I feel like a complete basket case, so I'm grateful for the distraction of having to drive home. I spend the time mentally composing texts — which I send when we stop for a brief break.

Sometimes having apprentice artists is a bit of a hassle, but in this case, the timing has worked out in my favor. I was about to set Delaney Jane and Kayden free to face the world on their own. Both are fully capable artists. They simply need a little more confidence and time in the chair before they feel fully comfortable. The good news is they are both available to cover for me indefinitely if I need them to. I'm a bit surprised by my dad's response to the whole situation, given the showdown we had earlier. I expected him to be far more explosive and upset. Rather than argue that I'm indispensable, he encourages me to spend the time with Declan and his family. When I express my surprise, he reminds me we only get one chance to say goodbye and if we miss it, we may never get it back.

When we pull up in the driveway, Declan slowly gets out of the truck and looks around as if he's lost. By the way he is holding his hands, I can tell he is searching for his beloved guitar. Since the mugging, he still struggles to play, but the habit is as natural to him as breathing and he clearly misses it. I walk up behind him and put my cheek on his back as I murmur, "Is there anything I can do to help? We should probably find some more comfortable clothes. We're probably a little overdressed for the hospital."

"I haven't figured out anything yet," he admits, raking his hand through his hair.

I hug him tightly as I reply, "I'm not sure this is something you *can* figure out. I think you can only cope with the news the best you can. Right now, your family needs you at the Mayo Clinic in Jacksonville, so let's get you there. That's the first step. We'll figure out what to do next later."

Declan pivots around in my arms and looks at me as if I'm some strange alien creature he's never seen before as he exclaims, "We? What do you mean? Don't you have to work? I didn't ask you to set aside your whole life for this, this is my mess!"

I trace my finger over the worry lines in his forehead as I respond, "You know, I always thought that was one of the nicest perks about being in a relationship. I get to do sweet things like this just because. You need me and I'm here for you — it's cool the way that works. Score one for being the girlfriend."

"Are you sure? Jett has clear ideas of how he wants things done and I'm not sure he'll be chill with you taking any time off right now," he worries.

"Declan, trust me. I've got this covered. Mom and Dad are totally okay with this. They are on their way to get Inkblot so they can cat-sit for us. I am covered at work for as long as I need to take. I'll reschedule any complicated pieces I have on the books. You are my most important priority right now."

Declan hangs his head for a moment, and I see him wipe away tears. I gently lift his chin with my finger. "I know it's hard, but we have to believe it'll be okay. He is in good hands at the Mayo Clinic."

"It's not only that," he explains, squeezing my hands. "For years, I admired your strength, compassion and artistry and I wondered what it would be like to have somebody like you in my life. Today, on the day you openly call yourself my girlfriend, I can't even celebrate this moment between us because my worst nightmare is coming true and I can't do anything to stop it. It's like the universe is laughing at me."

I pull Declan to me as I gently kiss him on the lips and murmur, "Luckily, I don't consider this girlfriend thing to be a short-term gig. I'll still be around after your dad is through this crisis and everything is back to normal."

It's a good thing I don't plan to tattoo for a while, because Declan is gripping my hand tightly enough to bruise my knuckles. The elevator ride up to the Cardiac Care Unit seems to be taking an excruciatingly long time. As we walk down the hall to the room, Declan is breathing heavily.

I stop in the middle of the hallway and back him against the wall and wrap my arms around his waist. "Everything will be okay. Whatever is going on with your dad, we'll work through it."

A look of pure dread crosses Declan's face. "Jade, I probably should've said something before, but there was more to my leaving home than creative differences with my family. At one point, I hoped to marry my brother's wife."

I ask the first question which pops into my head, "Recently?"

"Oh, God no!" he replies with a gust of air. "Rowan and I both dated Shannon in high school. I thought she was serious about me. She told me she only dated Rowan to make me jealous when we were fighting, but after I told her I wasn't cut out to take on the family legacy of my own car lot, she was a lot less interested in me and a lot more interested in my brother. Unfortunately, my emotions were still tied up in her and I blamed my brother for her betrayal. To this day, I've never been able to untangle the mess."

A thousand thoughts are spinning through my head, but finally I manage to articulate one. "Are you trying to tell me you're still in love with this woman?"

Declan shakes his head. "No — at least not any more than any other person who fell hard and fast for their first love and then was gutted by them." He gives a self-deprecating shrug. "I told you because it could get awkward and I wouldn't be able to explain unless you knew about what happened before."

"I don't know if the explanation is helpful because now I'll probably hate her on principle," I wrinkle my nose.

Declan hugs me tightly as he whispers in my ear, "J, I think that's the nicest thing anyone has ever said to me. Thanks for having my back."

Declan gives me a quick kiss, straightens his spine and grabs my hand with more purpose than I have seen since his brother called and marches into his dad's room.

From the moment we step through the door to the room, I can see why Declan might feel a little uncomfortable with his family. Immediately, several sets of eyes meet ours. They are varying shades of blue and every person in the family, including Declan's mom has a severe businessman's haircut. Hers has been softened a tiny bit, but essentially they all look like clones of each other. Declan with his sandy blond hair and hazel eyes looks like the odd man out. It isn't until his mother smiles softly and greets Declan that I see any real family resemblance.

"*A leanbh*, I'm so glad you're here." She gracefully stands up and gives him a hug. "Your dad is a tough one, but he can use all the support he can get. You know he's going to be upset you missed all the drama. He likes a big audience when he puts on a show."

Declan chuckles. "Mom, technically I'm the middle child. I never was your baby — that honor goes to Rowan."

I look down at the pale man lying in bed hooked up to every manner of machine. It is clear where Declan gets his height. The man, even in his frail state, looks like an unmovable mountain. His dark eyelashes are fluttering as he grimaces in his sleep.

"Oh for Pete's sake, where is the nurse?" a tall gentleman with dark hair and intense blue eyes complains, as he paces at the foot of the bed.

Declan's mom answers, "Finn, keep your voice down. Your father is trying to sleep and you are not helping. The nurse explained she doesn't have orders for anything stronger. She's working on it."

Declan's jaw tightens and I place my hand on his arm as I whisper, "It's okay, he's still asleep. It's likely soreness from his rib cage."

She looks at me as if she's just noticed I'm in the room. "Can I ask how you know this? Are you a nurse?"

"No," I answer as I shake my head, "I'm a tattoo artist, but I took care of my grandfather after his heart attack and he told me how sore his ribs were after his procedure."

I hear a snicker over in the corner as Declan's other brother quips, "I see your taste in women hasn't improved any over the years."

It's a good thing my hand is wrapped around Declan's bicep because he is seconds away from springing out of the chair. "This is about your dad, not your brother," I mutter under my breath.

I hear Declan expel his breath. "Nice to see you too, Rowan. How is Shannon?"

"Gone. She found greener pastures up the food chain," Rowan answers bitterly.

Declan blanches for a moment. "Sorry, man."

"Are you? You didn't even come to the wedding,

doesn't seem like you were a fan of us."

"Not that it matters now, but do you blame me?" Declan asks with an edge of sarcasm.

"I dunno, but I don't think you had to disown the whole family. They didn't do anything to you," Rowan argues. "You and I could've settled this like brothers. You didn't have to drag the whole family into it."

I feel Declan tense again but his voice remains level. "I'm sorry to disappoint you, little brother, but it wasn't all about you. In case you haven't noticed, I don't fit here. I never have."

"Did you try? Or did you decide the Stone lifestyle wasn't for you? Because that's what it looks like to us. Dad is in that bed because he has had to shoulder more than his fair share of the family business because you're off gallivanting around, feeling your bliss or whatever it is you do," Finn accuses.

"Enough!" hisses Declan's mom. She looks at all three boys squarely in the eyes as she threatens, "It might be a challenge, but if I have to, I will find three rooms and put you in them if you keep this up. Your father almost died today. Is it too much to ask for the three of you to stop fighting for five minutes?"

Declan stands up and walks over to his mom and kisses her on the cheek. "Sorry, you're right. Let me make a few introductions: Mom, this is my girlfriend, Jade Petros. Jade, this is my mom, Claire Ailín."

Claire unfolds herself and stands up to greet me. She is so graceful I almost feel compelled to curtsy. Even with a tear-stained face and red eyes, she is beautiful.

As I shake her hand, I say, "I'm sorry for the circumstances, but it's nice to meet you."

I cringe as the words fly out of my mouth, they seem so inane and stupid but I'm not sure what else to say. Declan hasn't talked a lot about his family. I don't have much else to go on, but I hate to talk in worn-out clichés.

"I'm sorry, but you have me at a disadvantage, I wasn't even aware Declan was dating anyone."

Something about the honesty in her words strikes me as funny and I start to giggle. You know, those giggles you get at church when you're supposed to be praying silently? My reaction is radically inappropriate because we're in the hospital. Everyone is looking at me like I'm a little nuts, but I can't seem to help myself. The harder I try to be circumspect, the more I feel compelled to laugh out loud. When I can finally contain myself, I try to explain, "I'm sorry, Mrs. Ailín, you weren't the only one taken by surprise by this relationship. I was too. Declan and I have been friends for many years. We didn't become more than friends until recently. Your son is a wonderful man, I'm sorry it took me so long to pay attention to that fact."

Much to my shock, a tear leaks out of the corner of Claire's eye and trickles down her cheek.

Finn shoots daggers in my general direction as he accuses, "Look what you did with your craziness, you made Mom cry again! I think you should leave. You're not part of this family." He narrows his gaze as he turns to Declan. "Why is she even here? We've never even met her. Why did you feel like she should be a part of such a private time for us?"

"Finnigan Shamus Ailín, I warned you once before. Keep your peace!" Claire warns. "You never even bothered to ask me why I was emotional."

"Mom, she was clearly making you upset," argues Rowan, as he defends Finn.

Claire throws up her hands as she responds, "Only in the best of ways! Jade here reminded me of what it was like in the earliest days with your father. Connor and I had no intentions of falling in love. He was the big, pushy kid next door — the one who always lost his basketball over the fence and drove obnoxious cars. I was interested in horses and books and much too shy for his polished good looks."

"What made you change your mind, Mom?" Declan asks, curiosity written all over his face. It's clear he's never heard this story before.

"Are you sure you want to hear this? It is the silliest story ever," Claire recalls, her smile indicating she's already lost in her memories. "Your Dad and I are from a tiny town in Vermont and went to a small Catholic school. Our school was something like you would see on one of those old-fashioned TV shows like *Little House on the Prairie*. All the grades were crammed together in one school. We had the lower grades in one building and the upper grades in another, and we all interacted for lunch and during our breaks. One spring when I was in the eighth grade and oh so sophisticated — or so I thought — a wave of chickenpox went through our school. When I say went through our school, I am not exaggerating, nearly everyone was affected, teachers included. They tried to contain it by making us stay home, but there were so many of us and it kept cycling through the school because it would pass from sibling to sibling. Finally, they made everyone stay home for a month and they sent a teacher around to each neighborhood and would teach groups of kids who had been exposed."

Finn looks at Rowan. "Can you imagine something like that happening these days?"

Rowan shakes his head and Claire continues, "My mom sent me over to your dad's house because there were more kids over there and it was easier on her. Your poor dad had the worst case of chickenpox I'd ever seen. His hands and face were so swollen it was impossible for him to hold a pencil or even see a book. I began reading the class material to him to help him out. Your dad was a slick one — even as a teenager — and soon he had me reading his detective novels and his comic books too. Before I met him, I hadn't ever read those kinds of books, but I found a few of them to be interesting and exciting. It didn't take us very long before we were talking about writing our own stories and plotting our own endings to the books we'd already read. It turned out the guy who I thought was shallow and vapid, loved books as much as I did and was incredibly fascinating to talk to. We stayed friends throughout the eighth and ninth grade. In the tenth grade he started dating Carly Sue Tarlington—"

"Uh-oh," I breathe under my breath, while hanging on to every word of her story.

"Uh-oh is right. I had to come face-to-face with the realization that somehow I had fallen head over heels in love with the kid next door. A guy who in many ways was my polar opposite. He was charming and outgoing — never knew a stranger in his whole life. And here I was afraid to talk to the priest in confessional because he was somebody I didn't know."

"Mom, that's so hard to believe. You deal with customers every single day. I've never seen you not interact with them. You are like the grand hostess of all the car dealerships. All those huge parties you throw at Christmas time … how do you do it if you're so shy?" Declan is completely incredulous.

"Funny you should ask, since you are the one who is most like me. When you were little, I took you to music lessons. I used to have to bribe you with cookies and candy to get you to perform in front of your piano teacher. You were so shy, I wasn't even sure you'd stick with your lessons."

"Declan was shy?" I ask, sure I misunderstood. "He performs in front of hundreds of people a week now. I can't imagine a time he was ever shy."

"It's true. I think Connor rubbed off on both of us. He used to make you practice talking to the salespeople like they were customers."

Declan chuckles. "That I *do* remember. I don't remember ever being shy around music though, I remember it being an escape for me and a feeling of freedom, but I don't remember being scared of performing. I must've gotten over my shyness when I was young."

Finn looks at Rowan and rolls his eyes. "Can you believe he doesn't remember beating the pants off me in the elementary school talent show after I practiced my magic act for six months?"

The look of astonishment on Declan's face is priceless as he responds, "No, I don't remember. Tell me you're kidding."

Everyone in the room shakes their head as Claire pipes up, "You were phenomenal. The newspaper even came out and took pictures of you. They compared you to a young Donny Osmond or Michael Jackson. It was as if you were a gifted child prodigy but it was too much too soon. You were only about six or seven. Unfortunately, the cameras freaked you out, and you didn't want to come out of your room for almost a month. We couldn't do anything to help — you stopped singing for a while. The only time you sang was when you were helping your dad detail cars and thought you were alone. You kept it so private. Other than that, no one heard you sing a note for two or three years. You wrote songs by yourself and then performed them in the privacy of your room or on the shop floor in the locked car. You used to use your stereo and your little electric keyboard to make little recordings. You never showed them to anyone. One time, I accidentally got to hear one of the recordings because I needed to borrow the tape recorder for an important meeting, and you'd left one behind. I kept it and played it for myself; it kept me company for years after you left home. Unfortunately, it broke a few months ago, so I didn't have anything left of you. It made me incredibly sad."

"Mrs. Ailín, did you know Declan is all over YouTube?" I openly brag. "He is getting to be a famous street performer. There are videos of him everywhere. Would you like me to send you the links? I have them saved in my phone. One of my favorite videos of him is an acoustic guitar concert he did after the Boston bombings."

"Please call me Claire; when you call me Mrs. Ailín, I feel like I need to look around for my mother-in-law. I can't believe I didn't think to look on YouTube for Declan's music — everything else is on the Internet. We use the Internet to help sell cars at the lot. I prefer the old-fashioned way, but finding his songs should be easier than arranging financing online, right?"

I have to smile at her technology phobia, it reminds me so much of Marcus because he freezes up at the very thought of having to touch the computer. The online appointment system we have is enough to induce a panic attack. "I'll be happy to show you how it works," I offer. "Declan even has an unofficial fan page."

Suddenly Mr. Ailín's eyes pop open and I'm looking into hazel eyes similar to Declan's as he whispers in a raspy voice, "'Bout time my boy sang a new song. So tired of that old one."

Chapter Twelve

Declan

Whoever said you can't go back home clearly hasn't met my mom. I swear she kept my pajamas from ten years ago. Jade won huge brownie points from me when she gracefully accepted them and then went about quietly exchanging them. She scoured the Internet until she found a nearly identical pair in my size not riddled with moth holes. She paid an ungodly amount of postage to have them shipped overnight.

Many things have changed since I was home. Jade and I are now staying in the little cottage behind the house where my grandparents used to live. Jade has been helping cook meals and do laundry while my mom is at the hospital with Dad.

In the meantime, I've been working with Rowan and Finn. Although the art of the sale remains much the same, the technology involved in each car is much different. When I left the business a few years ago, only the top-of-the-line cars had anything resembling navigation systems and emergency communication systems in them, now it all seems almost like standard equipment. Now people expect to have features like backup cameras and cars which park themselves during parallel parking. It's a whole new technology gamut I'm not overly familiar with because my own car is several years old. I'm worse than a green-horn salesperson, because I should know this stuff.

I cringe as the well-dressed businesswoman I'm assisting has to plug her ears when the panic button goes off on the car I'm showing her as I try to disengage the door locks. "I'm so sorry, ma'am. I'm not familiar with this model. Selling cars is more my dad's game. I deeply apologize. I am trying to get familiar with all the buttons. I must've made a mistake; give me a moment to figure it out, please."

The woman gives a snort of laughter and then giggles uncontrollably, holding her side. Finn stalks over to investigate the situation, glaring at me over the woman's head.

"Is there a problem here?" He shoots me a withering glance as he yanks the keys out of my hands and shuts the alarm off. He turns to the woman. "I'm sorry, we rarely hire such incompetent people. We're having a family emergency."

The woman shakes her head violently. "Oh no, I don't think he's incompetent. I think he's honest. I always get intimidated by salespeople who know how to operate every bell-and-whistle on a car from the get-go. I'm always afraid I'll never understand how to use it as well as they do. I thought it was perfect that this young man had the same kind of difficulties I have when I get a new car. I always feel stupid when I'm the only one who can't figure out a new device. Maybe I'm not the only clueless one on the planet. I like seeing somebody besides me struggle with electronics for once."

Finn fiddles with several more settings in the car and shoots me a dirty look. "I'm sorry my brother made it seem so complicated, it's very simple."

The woman seems befuddled. "Would it be possible for me to take a test drive?"

Finn grins widely. "Certainly, where would you like me to take you?" He sticks the key into the ignition and revs the engine.

The customer nervously gazes back-and-forth between us. "If it's all the same to you, I think I would rather ride with him."

It takes all the skills I've learned over almost a decade of performing on stage for me not to actively gloat in my brother's face. "That would be perfectly fine, let me go grab a set of dealer plates for this. I'll be right back," I duck into the little sales office.

As we pull off of the lot and around the corner, I trade places with the customer whose name I've learned is Juliet. Finn is not fond of this tactic; he thinks it opens the car lot up to too much liability. I think it's good business. How is a customer supposed to know if they want to own the car without driving it?

As I hand her the keys, she quips, "Whoops, I guess we better be careful not to set anything off. We would probably give your brother an aneurysm."

The corner of my mouth hitches up in a half smile. "Most people don't guess we're brothers because we don't look much alike."

"He talks like a big brother and your smiles are virtually identical. I wouldn't worry too much about his bluster. I feel more comfortable with you. If anything, you earned the sale today, not him."

I blush a little. "Thank you, I guess. Cars aren't my thing. I'm filling in while my dad recovers. It seems like I make a mess of things more than I help."

"Are you kidding? You are the only person I have dealt with on four car lots who didn't treat me like a ditzy blonde when I had questions. Normally if I want to ask about the different engine types or exhaust systems, the salespeople will try to divert my attention to the pretty leather seats or the Bluetooth sound system. Although those things are nice, it won't tell me what my gas mileage will be like when I commute to work," Juliet signals and turns the car back into the car lot. "I wanted a few basic questions answered so I could make an informed decision. You would be amazed by how remarkably difficult it is to get someone to look me in the eyes and give me a few concrete facts about their cars. Thank you for taking the time to treat me like a regular human being."

Juliet's answer takes me by surprise. I knew that attitude was common several years ago when my grandma tried to buy a car, but I had no idea things were still that way. Not knowing exactly what to say, I merely shrug. "I did my best to answer your questions, I'm sorry I'm not as knowledgeable about cars as my brothers. If you need more precise details, I can get Rowan or Finn to provide them."

Juliet smiles widely as she responds, "No, I think I have everything I need. This car runs nicely and has a great deal of get-up-and-go. It has all the things I'm looking for. I'll take it. I also want to make sure whoever your boss is knows you are the reason I chose to get it from Stone Central Motors."

"I appreciate that very much, but after my performance today, Finn will assume I coerced you into saying something. He'll probably believe I promised you a special discount or something," I joke with a wink.

I direct her to park next to the service bay and Rowan catches the interaction. He scowls at me before he opens the door and mutters under his breath, "You can't help but flirt with the ladies, can you?" His voice was quiet, but not quiet enough because Juliet starts to laugh.

Juliet raises her eyebrow at me. "I take it this is another brother?"

I nod as I reply, "This one is the younger brother, Rowan."

She gives him a brief appraisal. "Hmm, too bad. He's cute."

Rowan flushes red and then starts to stammer out a response, "Excuse me? Did you size me up and dismiss me without giving me a chance to say anything?"

Juliet shrugs. "Pretty much. Sucks to be you, huh?"

Rowan opens his mouth to speak but nothing comes out before Juliet resumes talking to me.

"Declan, I want to buy this car, but I'm in the process of moving. My company is opening a field office in Jacksonville so I'm commuting down to Cape Canaveral at the moment. I don't need to take an extra car. Can you guys hold onto it for an extra week until I can get stuff situated?"

"Wow, you have quite a commute. You must love your job."

"Trust me, I do," she grin widely

"Where do you work?" I ask

"I'm not at liberty to say, but you've probably seen my company discussed widely on the news, sometimes more than we'd like. Think young, curious billionaire who wants to see tourists in space."

"Wow, are you his personal assistant or something?" Rowan asks.

"No, you couldn't pay me enough money to manage that side of him. I'm your average, everyday rocket scientist."

At least this time, Rowan had the good sense to shut his mouth.

My dad looks exhausted. I haven't seen him look this bad since he was training for the charity boxing match to benefit the Catholic Children's League, way back when I was a teenager. This cardiac boot camp he's in is intense. The doctors told my parents this is the best way to get my dad back on his feet. He is complying with the doctor's orders this time, but he is not happy about it.

At the moment, Finn and I are trying to keep him distracted and entertained with a halfhearted round of gin rummy. However, I think it's an epic fail on all fronts. It's neither exciting nor distracting. The only person distracted is me. My dad throws a playing card at me to get my attention.

"You been smoking those funny cigarettes while you were away? You can't pay attention worth a darn anymore," my dad observes.

"No, I have a bunch of stuff on my mind." I pick

the card up and shuffle it back into the deck.

"You think you have a lot of stuff on your mind? The doctor wants me off of work about ten times longer than I figured. I thought they'd clean out all the gunk in my pipes and I could go back to work, but they want me to do all this rehab stuff, stress management and diet changes. Heck, they've got me seeing the doctor every single, stupid day."

"Dad, you came precariously close to talking to St. Peter at the pearly gates, you get that, right?" I say with more agitation than I intend to.

"Great job, Declan!" scoffs Finn. "The doctors want us to reduce Dad's stress, not add to it."

"Sorry! I'm just trying to be real," I argue. "This was scary."

"Don't you guys think I know?" my dad counters, "*My* chest was split wide open. I can't take a deep breath without a tangible reminder I might die with my next breath — which is why I need to ask you a favor, Declan."

My heart drops to the soles of my feet. To say this is out of character for my dad is not only the understatement of the day, it is the understatement of the millennium. My dad and I are as different as day and night, oil and water, up and down, forwards and backwards — well, you get the picture. As much as I have always tried to win his favor, I'm not like Finn. I don't seem to have the ability to think along the same lines as my dad. It's as if our brains operate differently. If you gave us identical puzzles, we would solve them differently. We might even see two completely separate puzzles. I can't remember a time in my life my dad has openly asked for a favor. If he ever allowed me to work with him, it was usually to teach me some sort of deep life lesson. You know, like my mom was telling Jade about overcoming my reluctance to interact with people or my shyness about being put on the spot. I have no idea what he needs to ask me, but the very thought of it makes me want to bolt. I could use Jade's calming influence right about now, but unfortunately she and my mom are out grocery shopping for a big dinner my mom is planning for whenever Dad gets out of the rehab center.

My dad drills me with an impatient look as he asks, "Son, I'm in the middle of talking to you — where did you go this time?"

"I guess I'm trying to figure out what kind of favor you need from me that Finn and Rowan couldn't do better. They tend to be your go-to-guys. I'm a little out of the loop. You and I have never truly been in the same loop," I shrug.

"Finn tells me you sold a rig today that's sat on our lot for a while. Nobody wanted it. It was too sensible to be sporty and had too many bells and whistles to be sensible. I don't know why the manufacturer sent it out to us, I guess they wanted to show everything that was possible, but I had a tough time with that one. Finn said you handled the situation well and reeled in a tough customer."

Honestly, I'm about to fall out of my chair from shock. There wasn't anything Finn did today to indicate he was at all happy with anything I did all day. If I had to guess, I figured he wanted to fire me on the spot. This is a revelation I was not expecting; even if he was proud of the job I did, I didn't anticipate he would tell Dad about it.

"Juliet was a nice customer. She was a little rattled

from the way she had been treated at other car lots. The fact that I'm a bit rusty and my sales pitch is a little uneven made her feel more comfortable," I explain.

"Whatever you did, it worked perfectly. She ordered upgraded tires, a clear-coat for the car and full warranty. We couldn't have asked for anything more," interjects Finn.

"In reality, I was flying by the seat of my pants. I haven't done anything with cars in a while. Even when I did work with the family, it didn't come as naturally for me as it did for you guys."

My dad gives a chuckle which causes him to cough and grab his ribs in pain. After he finally stops coughing, he shakes his head. "I don't think you remember your childhood very well. We used to call you 'The Closer' around here. You could talk almost anybody into almost anything. You were such a natural. People would believe every word you said. You could talk about the natural beauty of the line of a dashboard or the curve of a fender and people would hang on every word you said. We used to watch you in total wonder. It didn't matter whether you were talking to men or women, young or old — you had them captivated."

"Why do I remember this completely differently? I remember you, Finn and Rowan talking about the new models of cars and feeling like it was a completely foreign language. Or you would work in the garage and be able to communicate without speaking. I struggled to sort out whether we were supposed to be using standard or metric tools. You guys lived and breathed the car business on a cellular level; I could never compete. Being nice to a few customers could never make up for the fact that the car business doesn't run in my blood like it does for you guys;

on some level it almost feels like I'm an outsider. If I didn't look so much like you, I'd almost think I was adopted."

"Who's filling your head with all this garbage? Is it the Jade girl? You are so much like your mother it's scary. Have you heard your mother play the violin? She doesn't even need music in front of her, she can hear it in her head. She hears all the parts of the music. Before she had you kids, they wanted her to play in one of those orchestra groups, but she was too shy."

I throw my hands up in the air in frustration. "Why is this the first time I've ever heard this story?" I stand up and pace around the small cramped room. "Do you know what a difference this would've made for me as a teenager?"

"I'm sorry, you didn't seem to have any interest in real music; you wanted to listen to god-awful stuff that sounded like it was coming from the bowels of Satan. Father O'Toole warned us if we didn't discourage you from pursuing your passion, we would be sitting in our living room doing an exorcism in a few years — your grandmother got so scared we could not even talk about your music in the house."

"That's the reason you stopped all of Declan's music lessons?" Finn asks incredulously. "Wasn't over half of Father O'Toole's parish leadership asked to resign because of some inappropriate pictures involving children on the Internet? It seems to me they didn't have a lot of room to be judging a little Kurt Cobain."

I give Finn a little salute. "I had no idea you even knew who I listened to. I'm impressed."

"I was busy during high school, not stupid," Finn

retorts. "Besides, you had some of the most beautiful girls in the whole school tripping all over themselves to get your attention. It was hard to ignore your success."

I openly scoff at his assertion, "Okay, I know that isn't true. I couldn't even hold on to the girl I had. There was no one waiting in the wings. Everybody thought I was some overgrown beach bum who didn't know how to surf. They were not interested in my nonexistent record deal or concert bookings."

"You didn't see what went on behind the scenes; Rowan and I were forever fielding requests for your phone number. The longer and bushier your hair got, the more insistent those requests became," Finn replies.

"Now I *know* you're messing with me because we went to a private Catholic school and everyone used to hassle me for being out of uniform. They used to call me Jerry after the homeless dude from the *Down and Out in Beverly Hills* movies. Everybody thought I degraded myself because I made extra money by singing on the street corners and at bus terminals. The closest I ever came to any respectability was when Mike and Amy surprised everyone and got married. They asked me to sing at their wedding, remember? They got married at the beach and I took my guitar and got a little microphone system from a discount electronics store."

"I do remember," Finn acknowledges. "People wouldn't shut up about it. They thought it was cool. There were people who told me I should've filmed it for you and sent it in as an audition for *American Idol.*"

"So explain this: if I was so respectable, why did everyone hate me so much? I was practically pushed out of town. Everywhere I went, everyone was talking about me. People would cross the street to avoid having to be near me. It wasn't as if I was wearing pentagrams around everywhere."

Finn looks a little embarrassed as he confesses, "That probably has more to do with Shannon's best friend, Marabella, than anything else."

"What about Marabella? I never did anything to her. I thought she was a nice girl."

"You might change your opinion when you know what she said about you," Finn grimaces.

"Don't stop now. You opened this can of worms," I challenge when Finn pauses to take a drink of coffee.

Finn scrubs his hand down his face. "Remember, I'm only the messenger, okay? I wasn't the one who said all this stuff."

"How bad could it be? I dated Shannon years ago. I barely knew Marabella."

My dad shuffles the cards. "As I recall, it was awful. The police came and spoke to us, but you were away at camp during the time in question so you couldn't have done what she said and they let the matter drop."

"What *matter*?" I probe. "I think I met Marabella maybe two or three times. She had already moved away by the time Shannon and I started dating."

Finn leans forward in his chair and explains, "It seems Marabella was extremely loyal to her best friend. When you guys were feuding during your senior year, Marabella started a rumor you had tried to sleep with her little sister who has Down Syndrome."

"What?" I bellow. "First of all, I didn't even know Marabella had a sister. Second, I planned to marry Shannon, so I only had eyes for her. She was my first love,

I wasn't looking to cheat on her with anyone, let alone with somebody I didn't know. That's disgusting. Let me get this straight… You all thought this was true?" I question, struggling to wrap my brain around it all.

My dad and Finn vigorously shake their heads in denial. "Of course not! We knew you weren't capable of anything like that. It was all a smear campaign

"I don't understand why someone didn't tell me what was happening."

"Don't you remember what it was like back then? You and Rowan were fighting like two wet cats in a burlap bag. There wasn't a civil word to be had in the family. Your papa had just died and your grandma wasn't doing much better. Claire was crying all the time. Gas prices were crazy high and no one was buying new cars. It was all I could do to hold the family together. You weren't interested in talking to anybody, let alone hearing any explanations. If I could get you to come home and shower once every three or four days, it seemed to be a miracle. You showed up to school just enough to not get kicked out. I'm still amazed they gave you a diploma."

"It was a little awkward to be in school and see my little brother be all kissy-face with the girl I planned to marry. All my friends disappeared and I thought it was because they sided with Rowan. Now that I know there was something more to it, it makes things so much clearer. Dammit, I wish someone would've leveled with me way back then."

"I'm afraid I'm the one who needs to take the blame. Your mother wanted to spell it all out for you, but you were so hell-bent to get out of town, I was more than happy to let you go without telling you the whole story — I can see now it wasn't fair to you," my dad admits, looking dejected and sad.

His defeated expression makes me feel guilty. There is no proof it would've made a difference even if he had told me what was going on. I was more than a little stubborn back in those days and there's a good chance I may not have even believed him. A random memory pushes in. I glance over at Finn with a look of resignation. "Dad, you can stop beating yourself up. Finn did try to warn me and I blew him off. I didn't want to believe Shannon would turn on me, so I ignored anything which even hinted at the end of our relationship, even when it was flying right in my face. That's how she was able to date Rowan right under my nose. I refused to see it."

"It seems to be Shannon's true gift in the world. Rowan refused to see what was going on too. Right up until she left him for someone else," my dad observes dryly.

"That's sad. When we were kids, she used to be a decent human being with a kind heart. I wonder what happened?"

Finn rolls his eyes. "At this point I don't know and I don't care. She has sewn enough destruction in the lives of my brothers; I hope Karma bites her good and hard in the butt."

Finn's uncharacteristically blunt remark prompts me to laugh out loud. "Nothing like family to have your back."

My dad coughs and clears his throat as he says, "Speaking of the family, let's get back to the favor I need to ask you."

I shrug, trying to disguise my trepidation. "I guess, if you must."

CHAPTER THIRTEEN

JADE

ON ANY GIVEN DAY, deciphering Declan's text messages are an art form, but on days he is stressed or angry, it's almost impossible. Something has set him off today. He seemingly has forgotten the alphabet contains vowels.

As I balance a bag of groceries on my hip and carry it into the house, I ask Claire, "Any idea what has your son so tied up in knots he's practically speaking in hieroglyphics?"

"Oh dear! I was afraid that might be his reaction. Connie must've summoned up the nerve to ask him," she replies.

"Ask him what?" I probe.

"Connor's doctors think he needs a little more time away from the business to get his feet under him and feel better after the surgery. They asked him to come up with a contingency plan which would allow him to take a few more weeks to heal. Connor wants to involve Declan in the business. I know my son doesn't think he is any good at the car business, but he is. Even with the differences between him and Connor, Connie can recognize what a natural talent Declan possesses."

"What about Declan's other commitments?" I question.

"I wasn't aware he had other commitments. I was under the impression he was free to come and go as he wished," Claire comments, as she put the groceries away.

"For a guy who claims to be footloose and fancy free, his schedule is remarkably packed with commitments. There are a lot of people who count on him every single day. He's often over extended," I explain.

"Maybe he shouldn't worry so much about money," she remarks, as she shakes her head in dismay. "I don't know," she throws her hands up in the air. "Maybe the problem is he doesn't worry enough about money. I have never figured him out."

"Claire, I think we're having a miscommunication here — you would be so proud of what Declan is doing with his life if you only knew about all of it. Your son is one of the most remarkable men I have ever met in my life."

"He is?" Claire asks. "But aren't you worried about him? He told me he was staying at your house because someone beat him up because of his job. Is that true?"

"It is true; some punk kids jumped him on a city bus and he was there because he was working. But, the attack could have happened even if he was a lawyer, a teacher, or a doctor. The part of Declan's job you don't see is he generously gives hours and hours of time away to charities every month. He volunteers for my mom at the library and helps teach young kids who struggle in school how to write music and lyrics. He performs free of charge for a Children's Hospital and the Veterans of Foreign Wars. If that weren't enough, he helps my neighbor go grocery shopping twice a week because she's not strong enough to do it by herself. Claire, your son may not be very wealthy, but he is one of the richest guys I know."

Claire puts down the groceries she's stacking in the refrigerator drawer and she walks over and pulls me into a tight hug. "Jade, I can't thank you enough for telling me. If I can get Declan to tell me anything at all, he just swears he is eating enough and he is having a good time. He promises me someday he'll come home and have a nice home-cooked meal. He never tells me anything about what he's doing or who he's doing it with. I always knew he would be my child who would march to a different drummer. He always seemed to notice different things in the world. If we went on a walk, he would find the broken sticks, the sick birds, and the animals with no homes. With such a tender heart, I always wondered how he would make it in the world. It seems perhaps he's found a way to make it just fine."

"Please don't misunderstand, Declan works incredibly hard. I doubt I could put in the number of hours he does and face the repeated rejections he does day in and day out and still stay as positive as he does. I know it must be incredibly tough, but he seems to take it in stride. I think he was most worried about letting you and Connor down."

"I know my husband can be a tough one to please, but he is very proud of what Declan has accomplished. Many children Declan's age have given up. Connor is impressed with Declan's ability to follow through with his dreams."

I remember Declan's conversations with me about his parents, and I don't recall him ever referencing his father's approval. "Claire, does Declan know Connor is proud of him?"

Claire stops folding the grocery bags as she pauses to think, "Surely he does. Otherwise, Connor would never ask him to step up and help him with the business."

"I don't know if it's quite so simple, Claire. Something about conversations with our parents can make things so much more difficult. I'm in the middle of it all with my dad right now too. We can't seem to get ourselves on the same page about what's best for me. My dad grew up with a vision of me in his head and things have recently changed. I am no longer the little girl he imagined I would grow up to be and I'm not sure he'll ever fully adjust. I don't know how to bridge the gap between who I am and who he expects me to be. It has made communication between us difficult. I don't want to hurt his feelings, but I can't be the person he wants me to be. I'm not her anymore," I trail off, surprised I disclosed so much.

Claire hands me a box of tissues as she remarks, "Oh sweetie, I'm sorry. That is so incredibly difficult. If it makes you feel any better, I think the you that you are right now is thoroughly delightful."

"Thank you, that's incredibly kind of you to say. But, at the moment I'm concerned Declan might interpret Connor's offer as pressure for him to be more like Finn and Rowan and less like himself."

"Oh, I never thought about that. You're right, Declan might think Connor wants him to give up his singing. I don't think that's the case, but it might seem that way to Declan. I'll talk to Connor about it."

"I don't know, I could be entirely wrong about the situation."

"Knowing this group of hardheaded men of mine, I think you're probably right. If there are a hundred ways to interpret the conversation correctly and one way to misinterpret it, my guys will misinterpret it and probably get in a huge fight over it," Claire replies.

"They do seem to fight a lot. It must have been loud when they were kids."

"Have you ever watched tornado coverage on the Weather Channel with the volume blasting on high? That's roughly equivalent to what it was like around here."

I tuck my hand into Declan's and stick it in his deep jacket pocket as I snuggle closer. "I've never run away from home with someone before. How did you get away with it?"

Declan stops to pick up a piece of driftwood and throws it back into the surf. He shrugs. "I didn't leave them much room to argue. I informed them I was kidnapping you and I would return you in a couple of days if I felt like it. My mom has my number to get a hold of me if my dad ends up back in the hospital, but otherwise they're not supposed to even call me — this is our time."

"Wow, this may be a first in our relationship. I think we've always been accessible to somebody. We can be like an old married couple who vacations in a honeymoon suite for the first time without the kids," I joke.

All joking aside, it's kind of what it feels like. Declan and I have been so busy lurching from personal crisis to personal crisis, we haven't even had a chance to settle in and enjoy each other as a couple. In a way, this is our first little mini vacation.

"Only in Florida can we find a little seafood shack open on the beach in January," I remark, as we come up to a little shack with a grass roof and barstools.

"Hawaii too; one guy I used to busk with lived there for a while. He made good money, but he could dance the hula far better than me. I guess it pays to be multi-talented." Declan pretends to do the hula.

I laugh at his antics. "I don't know, I think you're talented." Looking around at the deserted picturesque beach setting and sampling my frosty, fruity drink, I wait a few minutes before I break the silence. "Is there any particular reason you ran away from home?"

He's a little surprised when I openly bust him. However, his chagrin doesn't last long and he grins sheepishly. "Wouldn't you?"

I knew all of this was taking a toll on Declan; I guess I underestimated how much.

"What can I do to help?"

"I don't know how much you can do. I feel like everything I believed about myself might not be true. I always thought I was almost completely to blame for the collapse of my relationship with Shannon, but now it seems like Rowan and I were both pawns in some game we'll never figure out."

"I agree. Whatever it was, it was a sick and twisted game," I commiserate.

"You haven't even heard the worst part of it yet. Her deception is far more reaching than I ever knew and involved her friends and family."

"I'm sorry she did that," I remark. "You guys deserve

better."

"The weird thing is trying to figure out how she changed my perception of myself. I always figured if I couldn't make it work with her, as hard as I tried, maybe I didn't have what it takes to have a real relationship. I spent years — and I do mean years — avoiding having any sort of committed relationship at all because I felt like I didn't have the interpersonal skills to pull them off. I know now my logic was faulty, but I remember thinking if I couldn't make it work with the woman who had captured my soul, who I thought about with every waking breath, what possible chance would I have with anyone else?"

"Wow! She did a number on you."

"That's the sad thing, it wasn't only me; it was the whole family. Because of all the garbage and my anger over it, I shut myself completely off from everyone who would've been a supporter. So, I left. I stopped talking to everyone. I made a lot of faulty assumptions. I figured no one in my family was anything like me or could ever support my love of music. It never occurred to me I might be wrong."

"How are you feeling about things now?" I ask.

"Confused, ripped off, angry, duped, embarrassed and ashamed for what I put my mom through. If I had been more honest about how I was feeling, maybe I wouldn't have felt the need to escape. I didn't realize my mom cared so much. It kills me to see her heartbroken. If that weren't bad enough, realizing most of this was based on a bunch of misunderstandings makes it a million times worse."

"I understand what you're saying, but I don't think

you can take all the blame on yourself. You weren't the only one who wasn't communicating clearly. Hindsight is a wonderful thing — if we could all live our lives knowing what we should've known, it would be much easier, but we can't. We can only make decisions based on what we know, not on what we wish we knew."

"I think you are way too quick to cut me slack. I was a huge jerk back then. I'm not sure a whole lot of people were sad to see me hit the road. Honestly, I can't say I blame them," Declan absentmindedly handles the gold money clip Connor gave him.

"I don't know a lot of teenagers who don't meet that definition. I wouldn't beat myself up over it if I were you. It seems fate has given you a chance to redefine yourself — even though the circumstances are not ideal, this gives you a chance to mend fences with your family while you help out your dad."

Declan looks up at me with a pained expression on his face. "I suppose you're right. Somehow I can't help but feel maybe this is another chance for me to completely lose sight of who I am. Am I a car salesman who plays a little music or am I a serious musician who happens to be selling cars?"

I jump off my barstool and stand between Declan's legs as I wind my arms around his neck. It never ceases to amaze me how much the two of us have in common. It seems like a lifetime ago I thought he was a carefree drifter who couldn't be bothered to find a real job. Now I know he is as stuck as I am — torn between the person he needs to be for himself and the person everyone else wants him to be.

"What if you are an amazing musician who is talented, thoughtful and gracious, while at the same time loyal to your family? I think it's okay to set aside your career to help your dad who is in a tight spot. I don't think it makes you any less of a musician at heart. I think it's entirely consistent with who you are."

"I'm so tired of trying to figure all this out. It's like the puzzle pieces don't match. It's not possible to make everyone happy," Declan declares with a deep sigh.

I lean over and kiss Declan, teasing his lips with my tongue before taking the kiss deeper. "I think we have the night off from solving the world's problems. You ran away from home, remember? We should take advantage of our time as fugitives. It seems to me we've got a pickup with a canopy and some sleeping bags and feather pillows. I brought some stuff to make s'mores and the beach looks deserted tonight. I don't know about you, but that sounds like the makings of a perfect party for two."

"I'm still amazed you drive a big 4x4; with your jet set life, I would've expected you to have a little sports car," Declan comments, as we walk back to my truck.

"Trust me, I did not escape the show-off stage, Dad has pictures of me in some atrocious miniskirts with a bright red Corvette convertible I was sure I had to get right after *Over It* hit it big. I thought I was hot stuff; fortunately for the world, my giant ego stage didn't last forever."

"I'm surprised Jett didn't like the Corvette," Declan comments with a grin.

The wind gusts and I have to stop walking for a moment. "I think that was part of the reason it was difficult for me to keep it. My dad did love it and Onyx would have too. My dad and my brother enjoyed working on cars together. It was their thing. Onyx would've gone ape over my car and the fact that he couldn't, made me cry every time I tried to drive it. Finally, I reached my breaking point and one day, I met a Make-A-Wish teen who had recently gotten his driver's license. I could not believe of all the things in the whole world he wanted to do before he died, he chose to come visit Ink'd Deep and hang out with me — so, when we went out to lunch and he caught a glimpse of my car and had an over-the-top reaction, I talked to his mom and gave it to him."

Declan pulls me back toward his side and kisses me on the top of my head. Most people would think this is a patronizing gesture but I've come to recognize that Declan often does this as a stalling gesture when he can't think of anything to say. We stand there for a few moments watching the waves crash against the surf before he says, "Jade, I don't think you get enough credit for being the most epic example of human generosity I've ever seen. I'd be willing to bet I'm the first person you've ever told that story to, right?"

Inexplicably, I blush. "Technically, no. I had to tell Rogue what I did because I needed a ride home."

"Did you tell Jett? That's not exactly something you could hide from him —"

"Have you seen Smoke recently?" I ask with a smirk.

"Yeah, the guy is running out of real estate for tattoos."

"Smoke has a plan to become one of those 'inked' fitness models. I've been trading him tattoo work for a vintage Harley my Dad is working on as a project bike. I think my dad believes I traded my car in for it. I never bothered to correct his assumption."

"So, that's why you nearly killed yourself doing his

back piece in one sitting?" Declan guesses.

I shake my head to confirm. "Mm-hmm. Smoke had a big photo shoot the next weekend and there was no way to photo-retouch his tattoo because it was so intricate. It was kind of an all or nothing undertaking."

"I reassert my contention. You are an epic human being."

"No more so than you," I counter, as we get to the back of my truck.

"Would you mind lifting the cooler and boxes out for me? I tweaked my shoulder when I was helping your mom with the groceries."

I'm insanely excited about what's coming next; it's been ridiculously hard for me to keep my secret. When Declan nods and pulls out his set of truck keys — yeah, it's crazy we exchanged keys to stuff a few months ago, we are like a truly domesticated couple now — it's all I can do not to dance like a kid on Christmas Eve.

In 3 — 2 — 1… I mentally count down as I hold my breath. "What did you do?" Declan asks suspiciously as he sees the very large box with his name on it. He removes the box from the back of the truck and sets it on the beach in front of me. I had forgotten how oversized the box is, Claire and I had to go to an appliance store to find a large box to try to disguise the gift. I wrapped it in *Peanuts* themed paper and placed a bunch of festive bows all over it. Grabbing one off the box and sticking it on the top of his head, I take a picture with my cell phone as I say, "It's a present, silly. I think most people open them."

"I thought Mom was planning a big party to make up for Dad missing Christmas. Don't you want me to open it there?"

"Nope. I have other presents for that day. This one is for just us."

"That's not exactly fair, I don't have anything for you. You said nothing about presents. You caught me empty-handed."

"Don't worry about it, *you* are my present. This isn't a competition. For the first time in years, I wake up with a smile on my face; that is priceless to me."

"I still don't understand why you got me a huge present. This hasn't been a very fun time for you. I've been gone all the time and sort of dumped you on my mom. I've been cranky and inattentive since my dad got sick; if anything, you deserve the presents, not me—"

This time, I can't help myself and I roll my eyes with impatience. "I'm sure I've explained this to you a dozen times before. I do nice things for people I love. I love you a lot, so I did a nice thing for you. Will you please open the box? Opening presents is one of my favorite things to do. I want to see if you like what I got you. I've been waiting what seems like forever to do this."

Declan's mouth opens in shock. "Do you realize what you said?"

I shrug nonchalantly. "Yeah? I love you. I thought we established that a while ago. I'm sleeping next to you at night and your toothbrush is right next to mine in the bathroom. I don't do that for just anybody."

"I didn't say you did," Declan argues. "But it feels a little different to hear you say it out loud."

I am a little baffled by his reaction because it never occurred to me that we've never said all the usual stuff people say in a relationship. We went from being friends to being inseparable. There never seemed to be any formal boundary lines between us. I didn't consciously not say the words; I guess I thought he knew.

"Different bad or different good?" I ask cautiously as I'm suddenly filled with dread. *What if he didn't want our relationship to go this far? What if he only wanted to be friends with benefits?*

Declan suddenly picks me up and spins me around. He is grinning from ear to ear. "Different good! Absolutely good, as in the best news possible. You made my whole freakin' year, Jade Petros. Now I'm glad I got mugged."

I gasp. "Declan, I wish you wouldn't say that. Those punks did such a number on you that you could've easily died. Even if it did mean we fell in love — I doubt I'll ever view it as a good thing."

Declan hugs me tighter and kisses me passionately before pulling away. "As much as the beat down hurt, if it was the price I had to pay to have you in my life, I would willingly pay it every single day."

My eyes tear up a little. "That's not exactly the declaration of love I always envisioned as a little girl, but it works for me." I kiss his jawline and rub the pad of my thumb along his bottom lip before I give him another kiss. "For the record you don't have to go around getting beat up for me, I like you in one piece without bruises."

Declan chuckles softly. "I'll take note of that, especially if I decide to busk on Charlie's bus."

"Now, please open your present before I collapse from impatience. I've always been terrible at this part of present giving. I'm one of those weird people who like to give presents almost more than I like to get presents."

Declan takes the bow off of his head and puts it on mine as he declares, "Maybe I won't even open this, maybe you're enough of a present for me."

I quickly try to snatch it off of my head and put it back on his as I screech, "Please don't do that! I worked so hard to surprise you with this. Don't ruin my surprise, please."

Declan chortles with laughter. "Come on Jade, I'm the middle child. Do you think I'd turn down the opportunity to get a present that's all mine? I don't think so!"

"Then quit stallin'! You're driving me crazy," I laugh as I push him toward the box.

It takes him a little while to get through all the wrapping paper and the two boxes we placed it in, but soon enough he reaches the prize. When he does, it's exactly the reaction I wanted to get. He is so into what he's doing he doesn't notice me taking a video of it with my phone.

He looks up at me with tears in his eyes. "You didn't."

"I did," I confirm. "I'm sorry it's not autographed by Roy Rogers like your old one."

"B-b-but," Declan stammers. "This is a Framus Hootenanny! John Lennon used to play this brand of guitar."

I shake my head excitedly. "It's a 1964. I thought about trying to get one John Lennon signed, but I decided I'm rather attached to having a roof over my head and food to eat," I explain.

"Yeah, no kidding," Declan exclaims with a surprised chuckle. "Museums can't afford stuff signed by John Lennon. Are you crazy? I can't even imagine how much you paid for this. I'm almost afraid to touch it."

"I took it to the University of North Florida's music department to have it authenticated before I bought it from this very nice retiring high school music teacher. Although they were very impressed and suitably reverent, they said it was an instrument which should be played," I disclose with an admittedly watery smile. Declan's reaction is everything I hoped it would be and more. The only thing that would've been better is if I could've located his original guitar. Unfortunately, an exhaustive search of pawn shops in Florida and surrounding states hasn't located it.

Declan sits and stares at the open guitar case for several minutes. He's mutely shaking his head. He gets off the truck bumper and walks aimlessly down the beach a few feet. I can see him tearing his hands through his hair. Of all the reactions I expected him to have, this was not one of them. He seems upset. I am at a loss. I thought he'd be thrilled. He is an unabashed music history buff and a huge John Lennon fan. When I found this gem, I thought I'd hit the gift-giving lottery. According to the experts, it's in practically perfect condition for an instrument so old. I don't even know how to process this. I thought he would unequivocally love it. I know it's not his old guitar, but still…

I'm lost in thought when he comes back and sits on the tailgate. He touches my shoulder and I about jump out of my skin. It is getting late and the sun is disappearing, but I can still see the intensity in his eyes as he asks, "Why?"

"I thought we covered the 'why' already," I answer, confusion clear in my voice. "I bought it because I knew you would love it and it would make you happy. I knew you were devastated when they took your other guitar and I knew you would totally appreciate the history behind this one. I bought it because I love you."

"Jade, you know most of the time I don't make very much money. I can't give you presents like this. I would have to save forever to get a guitar like this and even then, I probably couldn't afford it."

"Declan there's more to life than money and I don't know if I can ever adequately explain it to you but let me try —"

"Says the woman whose TV show went into syndication," he interjects.

"Fair enough, but even when I was bringing in big bucks, I didn't have what I have with you," I argue.

Declan's eyes light up with mirth. "Oh, there are so many ways I can interpret that comment."

I blush at the speculative gleam in his eyes. "In a different conversation, I might be talking about that, but not right now. What I'm talking about is the sense of peace I have when I'm around you."

Declan snickers as he retorts, "Yeah, right. I'm not sure I would describe what we have between us as peaceful. Haven't you noticed we tend to argue about every little thing from toilet paper to laundry soap and everything in between?"

I lift my shoulder in a half shrug. "True, we have our moments over the unimportant stuff. But let me tell you about the stuff which does matter: the stuff I keep buried so deep inside I don't even admit it out loud to myself very often."

"Am I going to need a drink for this conversation?" Declan jokes.

"Quite possibly," I answer honestly. "If you don't, I might. At the very least, we might want to get comfortable."

If I thought setting up camp would be enough of a distraction to postpone our difficult conversation, I was sadly mistaken. After Declan got the fire started and we returned to the truck and crawled into the sleeping bag, he turns to me. "I'm curious to find out how you see my presence in your life as peaceful. I feel like I've brought nothing but chaos."

"I don't sleep," I blurt, "or I didn't until you came into my life. For years after Onyx died, I was afraid to shut my eyes and go to sleep because every time I did, I would relive that day over and over."

Declan shifts uncomfortably beside me. "I don't know, maybe it's not me, maybe you just needed company or counseling or something —"

I chuckle dryly. "Trust me I've had copious amounts of both. Although counseling helps me a great deal, it's not the same."

"O-kay," Declan says slowly with a great deal of skepticism. "As you can tell from hanging around my family, I'm not the one with a reputation for being the most helpful person in the room."

"I don't know if I can explain it very well. It almost feels like I've been walking on a tightrope and since you came into my life, I've found solid ground and I can walk comfortably in my own skin again. I lost sight of who I was and what was important to me because I was so afraid of making people around me upset. You give me the courage to stand up for what I believe in and to remember what makes me whole. I love that you never try to change who I am."

Declan looks completely befuddled. "Change you? Why would I do that? I love you exactly the way you are."

Chapter Fourteen

Declan

Well, that sucks! The feeling that I could single-handedly cure cancer, fix the economy, solve the refugee problem and come up with a solution for global warming while living in complete domestic peace and tranquility at home with Jade lasted about as long as it took me to pull into my parking spot at work.

Seriously, I went away with Jade for a couple days to get away from my life, but I never expected it to be so spot-on perfect. It was the kind of story my grandfather used to wax poetically about when he would talk about meeting my grandma at the town dance hall. Apparently, she was a lot like Jade and pulled no punches either. Grandpa used to call her his firecracker. Sadly, I didn't know her well before her dementia set in, so I only saw glimpses of the woman he fell in love with. Still, until the day she died, he insisted she was the perfect match for him. Before now, I never fully understood his sentiment.

Jade has changed everything for me. It would be easy to explain it all away as good physical chemistry, but it's so much more. I run my hand down the elegant guitar case. It's such a visual representation of everything right about our relationship. Jade seems to be able to home in on what I need, but I'm unable to ask for. She knows what makes me tick. She knows the heart of me, sometimes better than I do. It's a scary thing to be so open with someone. It's liberating too because I don't have to hide anything from her — she already knows.

As I walk in the back office and place my new guitar in dad's office, Finn looks at Rowan and openly scoffs, "Look at Justin Bieber over here, he thinks he's going to have time to give us a concert. It looks like all that freestyle living in Gainesville has turned you soft. The rest of us have to work for a living."

"Get your underwear out of a twist, I had a rough few days, and I took my girlfriend away for a couple of days, cut me some slack. It's not like you guys are used to having me around anyway," I remark with a shrug.

"You are an idiot," Rowan grouses. "Keep your syrupy, happy self outta my face." He slams the refrigerator door shut with his foot and turns around and leaves the room.

I turn to face Finn. "What in the heck is wrong with him?"

Finn rolls his eyes at me. "It might have something to do with the fact that we've been up for about forty-eight hours straight working while you've been playing around. You promised to fill in for Dad, but we haven't seen hide-nor-hair of you."

"I thought senior management was covering for us this weekend," I reason. Even as I say the words out loud, they sound hollow to my ears. I sound like a twelve-year-old who forgot to get my paper-route handled. There is something about being around my brothers which makes me feel entirely incompetent to handle my own life.

"Welcome to the real world where plans change. You left before the directives came down," Finn says as if that explains everything.

"What directives?"

Finn's sighs dramatically. "Great, I suppose you don't watch the news either?"

"Usually I do, but this weekend I was too busy entertaining my girlfriend by the campfire, if you must know."

Finn grimaces. "Thanks a lot for that visual — as the perpetually single guy in the group, I totally didn't need that."

"Sorry man. You asked," I reply as I pretend to play a teeny tiny violin.

"No, I didn't, but the reason we're all fried is because there was another airbag recall and it impacted nearly every brand we carry. This one goes back six freaking years. It not only impacts the new cars, but nearly all of our certified used cars too. To make matters worse, every responsible car lot in the nation is trying to use the VIN verification tool to check the status of the recalls so the website crashes every two-point-five seconds. We finally gave up and started checking all the numbers by hand. Do you know what a pain in the butt that is? We could have used you, but once again, you completely let us down and disappeared."

I flinch.

Finn continues sounding more bitter with each word. "It was like déjà vu all over again. The only good news was Dad had several tests scheduled and they categorically would not let him out of cardiac boot camp. If it hadn't been for the follow-up testing, Dad would've been down here working his butt off."

I fiddle with my necktie and adjust my hair band as I let out a breath in frustration. "I told Mom to give you my emergency line if anything came up. I'm sorry if she didn't pass it on to you. I didn't mean to leave you guys shorthanded, but I had to get away and get my head screwed on straight."

"*Oh my Gosh!* Do you realize how many times I wish I could do that? But, I can't because I'm the oldest son. I'm always responsible. I think there are more days in the month when I wish I didn't have to get up and come to work and face another day selling cars than days I don't. I envy you so much for being able to escape the legacy. Some days it's mild jealousy, but other days it feels like downright hate."

The disdain in his words is stunning. I always assumed he loved the business as much as Dad. They talk about it all the time. Last I heard, Finn is slated to open his second large lot in a few months.

"Geez, why don't you tell me how you really feel?" I quip when I recover my ability to speak. Still stinging from his words, I ask, "Better yet, why don't you just do it? You're a grown-up. What's stopping you?"

"That would kill Dad for sure. I can't abandon the business that's been in the family for decades. Where would that leave Dad?"

"We still have one more brother and Dad hires good managers. That's what other car lots do. Most car dealerships aren't owned by a single family anymore. You don't stop being a member of our family because you don't work at a car lot. Stone isn't even our last name. Most people don't even associate it with us anymore."

Finn is silent for a moment as he steeples his fingers together in front of his chin. When he replies, his voice is rough with emotion, "You make surprisingly compelling arguments, Middle Brother A."

I smile at his use of my childhood nickname. "I gotta ask, what would you do with all of your new-found freedom?"

"Something … anything … without a desk and a multi-line telephone," Finn answers, as he sits at the large desk and untangles a long curly phone cord.

"Come on, that's not a career goal. That's a feng shui problem. What did you always want to do instead of selling cars?"

"You'll think this is stupid. It's way too late for me now. I've been out of school too long to make this happen, but I've always been interested in marine biology. I wanted to study dolphins and porpoises and save the manatees when I was in high school. I've always been fascinated by them. I wanted to be the person out on the Greenpeace boats trying to save them."

"You act like you are ten years older than me, you're like eleven months older than I am. Sure, we missed the five year high school reunion, but we haven't had our tenth year high school reunion yet; so don't be signing us up for the nursing homes quite yet," I tease.

"It feels that way. Most of the friends who I went to high school with already have degrees and a few of them already have graduate degrees. I'd feel stupid sitting in a freshman English class."

"I know for a fact you wouldn't be the only nontraditional student there. Jade is going back to school. She's our age."

"Why didn't she go to school? Too busy partying?" Finn asks.

"It's funny to me that you think just because she gorgeous she must be some sort of party animal. Truthfully, she's stuck in the same situation we are. She's been working at her family business since she learned to read and write and she'd like to be able to learn to do something else. Jade's facing a bunch of family pressure to stay exactly where she's at. If you'd taken the time to get to know her, you'd understand she feels a lot like you do."

"All I'm saying is she seems like she'd be the kind of woman who likes life on the wilder side," Finn argues defensively.

"Jade has her moments, but you'd be surprised about what makes her the most happy."

At that moment, my cell phone buzzes and Finn smirks at me as he remarks, "I can see she's already got you on a short leash. I never thought I'd see the day a tumbleweed like you would be tied down."

I'm only half paying attention to my brother's razzing as I try to process what Jade has written. Any way I read it, it's not particularly good news. I mean, I knew in the back of my mind this day would inevitably come; I had hoped it would be much, much further away.

Finn finally cues into my change of mood and asks, "Are you okay?"

I silently shake my head no as I answer, "I will be. Right now, I'm bummed. This day started out so well too. Somewhere along the way, the wheels came off of it."

"What's wrong?" Finn asks again.

"Jade has to leave," I answer bluntly.

Finn's eyebrows raise in surprise as he asks, "Why?"

"Remember all of those expectations I was telling you about? They've come back to bite her in the butt. One of the other tattoo artists has to have her wisdom teeth taken out. Since Rogue was covering for her, Jade has to go back to Ink'd Deep."

CHAPTER FIFTEEN

JADE

"I'm telling you, soda bread is one of the easiest things to make. It's virtually impossible to screw up," Claire insists. "Let me know if you want the recipe, I'm happy to share mine with you. Declan loves this recipe. He can help you since he knows how to make it. The kids have been making it forever."

"I don't know… I'm known for messing up baked goods. They're not my thing," I confess. "I think we've got all the recipes we need, what else do we need for the party this weekend? I can work on getting it together while you and Finn go pick up Connor from the rehab center."

Claire walks by me and pats me on the shoulder. "I'll sure miss you when you're gone. I like having you here," she remarks emotionally, before clearing her throat.

I like Claire and I'm touched by her emotion.

Claire looks through the cupboards but then points to the basement door. "I think all the serving dishes got put away with the Thanksgiving stuff. All that stuff is in a big box in the boys' 'Man Cave' as I call it. It should say, 'Company Dishes' on the box."

I nod. "Okay, I'll take a quick shower and get into my sweats. I want to try to shake this nagging headache. I'll take care of it later after I try to sleep this off. Go bring Connor home."

Claire sighs. "I'll be so glad to have him home, but it might take me a while at the hospital, I have to meet with the dietitian and a physical therapist while I'm there."

I have to laugh at myself and my shaking hands as I try to hold the flashlight steady on my cell phone. Darn my dad and his habit of making me watch horror movies with him as a kid. Don't get me wrong, I loved them too. But, it makes it a little scary to explore someone else's house — my imagination is a little more active than most people's. Wait… is that my heavy breathing? I hold my breath — no easy feat because my heart is beating a million miles an hour. No. I *don't* think it was me. *Crap!* It's always the woman who is home alone who gets murdered in these shows.

I pull my car keys out of my pocket and put them in my dominant hand and adjust the grip on my phone. I take a deep breath and let it out like they taught us to do in self-defense class so I don't pass out. I listen closely again and I hear nothing, so maybe I made it all up in my head. I sweep the flashlight around the room and I see a shadow reflected against the back wall that comes from my nightmares. I should probably do something or say something, but right now I'm stunned into total speechlessness at what I see projected in front of me: it's like my own personal horror movie. It is the silhouette of a man holding a handgun to his temple.

A strangled, horrified gasp escapes my lips as I try to utter the word, "Stop."

The figure in the black leather chair spins around and much to my horror, it's Rowan wearing an old baseball hat with a logo so worn I can't even make it out. When he recognizes me, he makes a wild gesture toward the door using the revolver. "Get the feck outta here. I'm not gonna have no check… no… I mean chick of Dec's mess my plans up again."

"What plans are those, Rowan?" I ask cautiously. "Having yourself a little party down here?"

He holds up a bottle of Jack Daniels that's alarmingly two-thirds empty and says, "Yup, me and JD here are becomin' real good friends with Mr. Peacemaker."

My heart about stops. Great. Rowan is, at best buzzed and at worst, flat out drunk. He's waving around a gun like it's an American flag at a Fourth of July picnic.

"Hey, you got a bunch of bullets to go in that Peacemaker? My dad's got one at home, but he accidentally ran over it with his Harley, so it doesn't work quite right and he can only load four bullets in it. How many do you have in yours?"

Rowan snorts at me as he laughs and says, "I thought my stupid big brother said you were smarter than our witch of an ex. Everybody knows it only takes one bullet to kill yourself."

"That doesn't sound like much of a party to me, why are you trying to kill yourself?" I ask as I carefully text #912 to Declan, holding my phone down by my side where hopefully Rowan won't notice it. Declan and I set up our system several months ago when he started worrying about me working late hours at the shop. I informed him I couldn't dial 911 every time I got a little scared of the shadows. So, he told me to dial #912 if I ever needed him to come rescue me like a knight in shining armor.

Right now, Rowan isn't paying much attention to me at all. He is too busy raging at the ghosts in his life, past and present. Rowan sits up in his chair and for the moment, sets the gun down on the computer table in front of him. I make a calculated gamble and re-send the emergency signal to Declan. I have no idea whether it went through because I've turned off all the notifications from my phone.

"You wouldn't know anything about what I'm going through because Declan is perfect all the time. The sensitive one, the artistic one — the one Shannon wanted to be with … but she settled for me. Don't think I didn't hear about that every d-darn day we were married. Now look at him —" he continues after taking a swig of alcohol. "He comes w-waltzing back home, but is he s-s-sorry for the c-crap he put everyone through? Oh heck no — he walks in like he owns the place. He kicked me out of my place on the showroom floor like he hasn't been gone all these years. I'm back in the r-repair shop like I'm some flunky who can't close a sale. I'm not like Finn, Dad will never give me my own lot and now Finn is about to have two. Nobody cares if I'm even in this family, I should end it all and make everybody's life easier."

I draw in a deep breath as his intent becomes clear.

"I can't take being a failure anymore. My wife doesn't want me, my family doesn't want me in the family business, even the people I hang out with online to play video games with don't want me around anymore. They say I'm too competitive and don't play by the rules. Some of them said it's not fun to play with me anymore. I mean how pathetic do I have to be to not be able to make Internet friends? Creepers who take children for sex slaves make friends on the web. I'm sick of it all. I'd rather not be here; there isn't anyone around who would miss me. I'm tired of pretending I'm okay when I'm not."

"That's not true," I challenge softly.

"You don't know anything!"

"I know quite a bit. You'd be surprised by what I know about video games. My business partner and his brother-in-law practically own an arcade. Tristan Macklin invented more than a few of them himself."

"Now you're full of crap, there's no way you know *the* Tristan Macklin," Rowan replies skeptically.

I shrug. "That wasn't exactly what I was arguing with you about … but if you boot up your computer, I can pull him up on Facebook."

Rowan scoffs. "Anybody can bring up his corporate site; it's a matter of public record."

I sigh. "What would it take for you to believe I know him?"

Rowan practically sneers at me. "Photographic proof — and not the Photoshop kind. I want the real deal."

"Video or stills," I ask.

"Yeah, right. You're stalling."

"I need you to boot up your computer so I can get to the website," I instruct.

As he goes through the boot up ritual for his computer, I get close enough to the revolver to see it is indeed a six-shooter. I am trying very hard to keep my breathing pattern normal, so I don't let him know how stressed I am. It's difficult to act like nothing is out of the ordinary when things are so desperately wrong.

After he opens the Internet browser, I make a move to sit down at the keyboard to type and he scowls up at me as he announces, "Nobody touches this computer except me. Nobody!"

Trying not to allow the fear in my voice to seep through, I carefully spell out the Internet address to Ink'd Deep and then show him how to navigate to the wedding album we added for Rogue and Ivy. I say a strong mental prayer because the girls' father, Isaac Rogan, has been messing around with the site to make it fancier and I hope it's functional. Never have a few wedding pictures been more important.

Fate appears to be on my side because the splash page for the site is a huge panoramic shot of the whole wedding party including me, Jessica and Jessica's grandfather, Walter. Not only are there pictures of Rogue and Ivy's wedding on this page but Rosa and Isaac's as well.

"Wow! I guess you do know him — unless you were a wedding crasher."

"Go to the third video down. It's kinda long because Marcus got a hold of the microphone and you have to know him, but he can talk for a while. Turn up the volume because the audio is kind of crappy and it's hard to hear over the background music, but if you listen closely, you can hear Tristan say my name and talk about me — it's kind of embarrassing, but he does."

Whatever I said, it must've been the right thing because Rowan is now completely absorbed in the hokey reception video. He doesn't even notice when I step back and remove the gun from the other part of the computer desk. When everybody starts dancing and giving toasts, he turns up the volume some more. I take the opportunity to open the latch on the cylinder of the gun and swing it to the side so I can see all six openings. He's right, there's only one bullet. I carefully turn the gun over and let the bullet fall out into the palm of my hand. Right about the time I close the cylinder and place the gun back on the computer desk, Rowan laughs loudly at something Marcus said on the videotape and I about jump out of my skin. "Is your friend always this crazy or was he drunk?"

"Honestly, I don't remember. But that's basically Marcus all day, every day. He is my partner at Ink'd Deep."

"You sleep with him?" Rowan blurts.

"Eww! No! Do you sleep with your coworkers?"

"No! In case you haven't noticed, I work with my family," he snaps.

"So do I. Marcus started working for my dad when he was a teenager. We grew up together. He's like my brother. He's married to Ivy. Ivy is Rogue's twin. Rogue is one of my best friends and Tristan's wife."

"You mean he's not just some rich client you tattooed?" he inquires. "I thought you were posing to show me how rich and powerful you are and how much of a loser I am."

"Nope. He's like my family."

"That completely blows my mind. He looks completely different from his gaming avatars."

"He's nothing like the world expects him to be. None

of us are. Tristan isn't the only thing you're wrong about."

When the video ends, Rowan clicks through some other close-up pictures of Tristan and Rogue. I take advantage of his distraction and tuck the bullet into the ankle of my shoe. He catches my strange movement and asks, "What are you doing?"

My heart pounds. "These Velcro straps drive me crazy. They never stay tight enough." I try to roll my shoulder nonchalantly.

He seems to accept my lame explanation as he looks back at the pictures on the computer. Finally, he turns back toward me. "What do you mean? What else did I get wrong?"

"You told me if you disappeared off the planet no one would miss you. You're wrong. I'd miss you." I lay everything on the line.

Rowan spins away from the computer screen and turns his gaze at me as he demands, "Yeah, so? What difference would that make? You're my brother's girlfriend, not mine. I don't want to deal with his leftovers again."

I raise my eyebrow dismissively. "If this Shannon chick was dumb enough to let not one, but two Ailín brothers slip through her fingers, that's on her. I don't see how that's your issue."

Rowan chokes back a laugh. "You might have a point."

I walk over to the little mini fridge and pull out some water and toss him a bottle. "Sorry, I've nursed Marcus through a few too many hangovers, this is kind of a habit. You'll thank me in the morning."

A look of total confusion crosses Rowan's face. "Did

you forget the part of this conversation where I'm not planning to be here in the morning?"

I hop up and sit on the desk as if I don't have a single care in the world, but in reality, my heart is in my throat. "Yeah, I wanted to talk to you about that."

"What could you possibly know about what I'm going through?" he growls.

As if an invisible thread ties our hearts together, I get off the desk again and silently walk toward him and squat down beside his chair. I grab his hands, right around the water bottle as I whisper in a broken voice, "More than I ever wanted to."

I look up into his face from my kneeling position beside his knees as I silently plead for him to listen.

"I know you are not my brother, but you're *somebody's* brother. You're also somebody's son, somebody's best friend, somebody's next door neighbor, somebody's work buddy, somebody's ex-lover, somebody's former student and someone's secret crush. If you decide to kill yourself, it might be the end of your problems, but you will forever change the lives of all of those people."

"You lie. I don't think that many people would even notice I'm gone," Rowan stubbornly argues.

"Rowan, I can tell you that's not true. I used to know somebody who sounded an awful lot like you. He was having a tough time in his life and he thought it would be better not to bother anyone with his problems. He told himself he was all alone and no one would care what happened to him one way or another. He considered himself to be an adult and too cool to be loved by his family. He got the idea that if he was only strong enough, he could handle everything all by himself. He figured somehow it was weak to ask for help." I have to stop and catch my breath and wipe away a tear.

Rowan leans forward in his chair, considering every word as he asks, "What happened to him?"

I suck in a large breath before I continue, still hard to say these words out loud even after all of these years. "He killed himself."

As much as I try to tell the story, my emotions bleed through every syllable. It's no less shocking every time I say those words out loud. I swallow hard and search Rowan's face for clues to see if he understands.

Rowan silently mouths the word, "Wow."

"Yeah, that sort of sums it up," I reply. "His pain may have ended that day, but I was given a life sentence of pain. Everything I knew to be true in my world became a lie."

"What do you mean?" Rowan asks me with wide eyes.

"My big brother is no longer always in my corner; I'm not anyone's sister anymore. My dad isn't a tough guy who never cries, my mom doesn't know how to answer the question of how many children she has, and I can no longer say my brother never kept any secrets from me — because, in the end, he kept the very biggest one of all away from me."

"Oh God, Jade I am so sorry. I'm sure he didn't mean to hurt you," Rowan apologizes, as his expression grows pale.

"Rowan, that's exactly what I'm saying — I never got to have this conversation with my brother. I'll never know what he meant to say to me. I never got to beg him to stop. I never got to tell him how much he meant to me and how much I would miss him every single day of my life. If I hadn't been so pushy about helping your mom with dinner tomorrow, I might've missed a chance to have this conversation with you too and I'd be left to explain to your parents … and your brothers … and your friends … and neighbors … and your coworkers … and the kids down the street and the news media … and perfect strangers who don't understand why you made the decision no one who hasn't been in your shoes could possibly understand."

I know my words are blunt and harsh, but I'm on a roll and I can't seem to stop them from tumbling from my mouth. For now, Rowan is sitting there in stunned silence. So I continue, "Let me tell you, there isn't any amount of time, or space, or counseling, that makes any of this make any sense. Sure, I can make rational sense of it in my brain. I can understand my brother was probably depressed and maybe under the influence of alcohol and perhaps bullied by his classmates — but in my heart, I don't know if I'll ever truly understand why my brother didn't reach out to me and ask me to help him through what he was going through. For the rest of my life, I will always have two hearts of Jade. The one that was there when Onyx was still alive and the shattered one which remains now."

Rowan visibly grimaces as he takes a swig of water and waits for me to finish.

"I've told you my story and for whatever it's worth, I beg you not to do that to the people around you," I plead, squeezing his hand.

A flash of anger crosses Rowan's face as he says, "Okay I get it, you think I'm a selfish son-of-a —"

"No! I—" I start to protest.

"Do me a favor: shut up. I listened to you, it's your turn to listen to me," he snarls.

My mouth drops open in shock before I finally compose myself enough to close it.

"Look, you threw some hard truths in my face. I still have to deal with that. Now, let me throw some back at you. I'm still twisted feckin' sideways. Just because we had this little talk doesn't mean I miraculously feel better. My life is still a monstrous claustrophobic mess I don't know how to deal with."

"Fair enough," I answer, letting out the breath I've been holding. "Want some help?"

"Honestly? Not from you," he answers sardonically. "Right now, I can't decide if I even like you. In fact, I might even hate you a little."

I stand up and kiss him lightly on the cheek as I announce, "You know what? I can live with that because you'll be here to live with it too."

Rowan chuckles wryly as he salutes me. "Touché."

Abruptly, he reaches over and flips on a lamp. A whole quarter of the den is filled up with light. He raises his voice and announces, "You guys might as well come and join the party, you've been sitting out there long enough."

CHAPTER SIXTEEN

DECLAN

STRAIGHT UP, HONEST TO God's truth: I'm shaking like a Chihuahua in a snowstorm. I've faced a few dicey situations as a street performer, but I have never witnessed something as scary as that. For kicks and giggles I'll throw in the time I was beat up and the time I was caught in the middle of a gang war in Miami — and I've still never been this flat-out terrified. Now I understand where Jade earned her nickname, "Ice." From the outside, she looks cool as a cucumber, although, I can tell from the way her left eye is twitching she probably has a massive migraine. She rarely ever says anything about her headaches; I have learned to interpret the subtle signs.

I can tell from the way Rowan shakes his head after she teasingly kisses him on the cheek that he has fully changed his mind — at least this time. The immediate crisis is likely over. Although I'm not super excited that there is still a gun a couple of feet from my girlfriend. As I glance at the gun with trepidation, Finn sees my intent and secures the weapon. He spins the cylinder and discovers there are no bullets. He yells out at me, "All clear!"

Rowan looks shocked as he demands, "Where'd my bullet go?"

Jade shrugs. "I secured it for your safety."

Finn, Rowan and I simultaneously roar, "You did what?"

Jade balances on one foot while she toes her shoe off with the other. She flips her shoe over and hits the bottom. I watch in amazement as a bullet falls into her palm.

"When the hell did you do that? I was only three feet away from you the whole time!" exclaims my brother.

"That's true, but you were also making good friends with Jack Daniels and got a little distracted. I know my way around guns, so I have the ability to be a little sneaky."

"Thank God Jett taught you to be tough. When Tristan was teaching the self-defense class, your dad bragged about you being like Annie Oakley, but I thought he was kidding."

"You're even crazier than I am. I could've hurt you with that thing. I'm not exactly in my right frame of mind these days," Rowan confesses in a shaky voice. He looks helplessly at Jade as he asks, "Why would you take that kind of risk?"

"Simple: I care about what happens to you. I truly do." Jade sways on her feet.

Rowan is closer to Jade. He catches her half a beat before I do. "Are you okay?" His voice is heavy with concern.

Jade nods carefully as she responds, "Yes, I'm fine. I just have a killer headache. If you'll excuse me, I'd like to lie down."

I quickly glance over at Rowan. "You gonna be okay here?"

He nods tightly. "Yeah, go take care of your girl. She doesn't look so good."

Finn touches me on the shoulder. "Go."

Jade shrugs us both off with a heavy sigh as she explains, "Guys, I have another one of my stupid headaches. I get them all the time. No need for me to call the 'whamulance'. I'm going to go take a couple of Advil or something and crawl in bed with a bag of frozen peas, okay? No need for all this drama. Seriously, you guys need to talk."

Jade turns around and heads toward the door. I'm tempted to follow her, but I know she would rather I spend the time with Rowan. As difficult as it is, I stay put.

As soon as we hear the door slam, Rowan turns to me. "Your girlfriend is fierce."

I look at him with narrowed eyes. "I hope you mean that in the most respectful sense."

"Oh, I have nothing but mad respect for Jade now," Rowan clarifies. "I admit when you first brought her around, I wanted to hate her because of what Shannon did to me."

"Me too," interjects Finn.

"She was awesome to me even though I went and made a complete fool of myself and dredged up all that stuff with her brother. She could've kept it all private and not bothered to try to help me — but she did, even when I was a jerk. If that wasn't enough, she put herself at risk to keep me safe by taking away my weapon, in my mind that makes her bad-ass."

I nod. "If you could only see the private side of her, you would respect her even more. She hides so much of what she feels. I don't know what I would do if I was in her shoes." I look directly at Rowan. "Did she tell you she was the one who found her brother after he hung himself in his dorm room? Did she happen to mention she barely sleeps? Or that in some ways her dad hasn't forgiven her for not being her brother? Yet, she is the kindest person I know. When I was hurt, she didn't think twice about taking me in and taking care of me."

"Yeah, some people are like that. Let me guess? She posted all over Facebook about what a wonderful person she was for doing all those great deeds for you," theorizes Finn sarcastically.

I swing my head around to glare at him. I'm sure there must be a story there somewhere. I wonder what I've missed in the time I've been gone. "Cynical much? To answer your question — she didn't post a thing. I don't think she even told anyone we were staying together."

"Congratulations, you must've found the one woman on the planet who doesn't live her life on social media. That's like finding a freaking magical unicorn."

"I'm not gonna argue that she's not magical. I haven't been this happy in years and I'm here, aren't I?"

"I have to admit, I'm surprised to see you here. I never thought I'd see the day. How did she accomplish that?" Finn asks.

"Let's say she helped me put things in perspective and helped me have a little faith in myself."

Rowan takes off his cap and runs his fingers through his hair. He throws the baseball cap onto the old couch and takes a swig of water. "She is good at changing your perspective, that's for sure."

"Rowan, man, I know we're tough dudes and all and we don't usually talk about all this stuff. But we are the Brothers A. I can't be the Middle Brother A unless you're the Little Brother A. We need to take care of this so you're safe."

"What am I supposed to do? Call somebody up and say, 'I need help because I want to hurt myself?' I'd feel stupid."

Finn clears his throat. "As Big Brother A, I think that's totally what you need to do, I can help you if you want. Why don't I stay here in the cave with you tonight? We can go talk to Dr. Murphy tomorrow morning. He's known you since you were a kid, if anybody can figure out what's going on, it's probably him."

"I guess if I have to talk to anybody about this, it might as well be him. He's a nice guy. Do we have to tell Mom and Dad about this right now? They've got enough stuff to deal with."

"Let's see how tomorrow goes and make decisions then," I suggest.

I walk over to Rowan and give him a tight hug and confess quietly, "I'm so glad Jade was here for you. By the way, you *were* wrong. I would've noticed. I would've noticed a lot if you weren't in my life; I would've missed you every single day. I know I don't say this enough, but I love you, Little A."

There's nothing like a near-death experience to make you realize all the things you've left unsaid with your family.

Finn, Rowan and I had a lot of years to make up for and many unfinished conversations between us. It's several hours later before I finally cry "uncle" and go back to the little cottage behind the main house where Jade and I are staying.

I expected Jade to be sound asleep at this hour; I'm alarmed when I find her curled up in the fetal position in the middle of our bed. She is clutching a bag of frozen vegetables. She has one shoe on and one shoe off. Alarmingly, she is not speaking to me at all; she's shaking and rocking, the rhythm broken only by soft moans of pain. Desperate, I get into bed behind her and pull her gently to my chest. That movement seems to startle her out of her haze of pain. When I see she's placed the garbage can on the bed, things become clearer.

"Migraine?" I whisper.

She places her finger on her lips asking me to be quiet as she carefully nods.

I have a few friends with headaches, but Jade's are worse than anyone's I've ever seen. Whenever I try to talk to her about them, she dismisses my concerns. She says they're due to stress, hormones, or her emotions. They might be, but still it seems like she has them all the time. I wish I could do something to take away her pain.

Helplessly, I hold her in my arms until she stops shaking and we both fall asleep. My nightmares are terrifying, but the disorienting thing is they're not more horrifying than what's happening in my real life.

CHAPTER SEVENTEEN

JADE

CLAIRE'S NERVOUS ENERGY IS radiating off her like light from a glow stick at a rock concert. She is working exceptionally hard to pretend everything is perfect and absolutely normal when it's clearly not. It only takes one glance at the empty spot at the dinner table to understand the impact of Rowan's absence. No one seems willing or able to talk about what's happening with him — even I feel stuck. As a guest, it's not my place to make sure everyone works through their feelings. On the other hand, acting as if nothing happened and Rowan merely stepped out to get the newspaper clearly isn't helping things. Claire looks as if she could burst into tears at any second.

The tension grows as we set the table in silence. Finally, she looks up at me with tear-filled eyes as she asks, "I don't understand why they wouldn't let him come home for dinner? We're celebrating Connie's discharge from the hospital. Why couldn't he come home for a few hours? It's like they have him locked in jail or something. He didn't do anything wrong!"

"No Claire, he didn't do anything wrong. In order for him to get help, the doctors have to monitor everything.

They've been putting him on different medications and having the psychologists and psychiatrists talk to him a lot. He's been bombarded with all sorts of different questions and different medications. It's a lot to take in. They have to treat him in an isolated environment so he doesn't get overwhelmed. This decision isn't personal. I know it feels that way, but it isn't. They make those decisions for his safety and the family's. Holiday get-togethers under the best of circumstances can be very stressful. He is in the safest spot right now, you have to believe that."

Claire pulls out a dining chair and slowly sits down in it. "Jade, I'm just so sad. My baby thought it would be better to be dead than to live one day longer. What kind of mom does that make me? I had absolutely no idea. He didn't even want to tell me about it. My child used to tell me everything!" Claire cries, wiping away tears. "Why would he stop when it really mattered?"

I also pull out a chair and sit down. I grab her hands across the table and squeeze as I say, "Claire, there are no great answers to those questions. I know my mom asked those very same questions after my brother committed suicide. They haunt her dreams. They haunt mine too. Onyx and I were freakishly close — people often thought we were twins. We could finish each other's sentences. Unfortunately, it seems he left off paragraphs and pages of his life. I thought he was having fun in college. He would send me funny updates and pictures. On the surface, everything looked fine. I didn't know to look deeper."

Claire swipes at the tears falling as she asks me, "How do I ever forgive myself for missing all the signs? If you hadn't been here, my baby might be dead."

Her desperate question lands with the force of a physical blow. "I don't know the answer to that," I whisper hoarsely. "If you ever find out, let me know."

"I can't believe you made me an apple pie without the crust," grouses Connor, as he practically licks the pattern off his plate. "What's this frozen yogurt stuff? I like homemade vanilla ice cream, you know the one made with pure cream?"

"I know what you like, Dear. But, that's what got you into this mess. I just got you home from the hospital. I'd rather not have to take you back right away. I'm following exactly what the dietitian told me to make for you."

Declan smirks. "Dad, it doesn't seem like you like this any less."

"Truth be told, you're right. Still, I don't like anybody telling me what I can and can't eat. I'm old enough to choose my own food."

"Connor, you listen here. The night we spent all those hours in the waiting room waiting to hear whether you would live or die are the scariest I've ever lived through in my life. I never want to do it again. So help me God, if I have to, I will feed you lettuce and turnips for the rest of our lives," she threatens.

Declan laughs out loud. "Watch out! She's pulling out the big guns now."

"Claire, now you know that's not funny. I hate turnips," Connor whines.

"I know you do — so do I. But, if that's what I have to do to keep you safe, I will. Don't complain about what

I cook for you — I'm only doing it for your own well-being."

"You're right, dinner was delicious. I shouldn't be complaining, especially after all that hospital food," he responds apologetically. Much to my dismay, he turns to me and says, "I noticed you didn't eat much, is there something wrong with your food?"

Nothing like being publicly busted. I've been spending the last forty-five minutes pretending to be invisible. I didn't want to ruin Claire's dinner because she's been working on it for days. She's probably been planning for many years for the time her family would be reunited. I didn't want to let a freaking migraine put a damper on her day. She's already stressed out enough because Rowan isn't here. Consequently, I've been gamely hanging in there. It's not easy because the smell of food makes me profoundly nauseous. Any movement or sound is enough to make me want to cry.

"A little headache," I admit, in a colossal understatement. "It tends to take away my appetite."

"Seriously? Again?" exclaims Declan in a frustrated growl. "They must be able to fix those somehow."

Finn begins clearing the dishes off the table. "I'm sorry, those must be awful," he comments as he tries to rearrange the dirty pans beside the sink.

Suddenly, the huge stack of pans falls on the hardwood floor in an avalanche of earsplitting sound. I cry out in pain as my stomach revolts and my vision goes black.

What is that awful smell? What am I doing sitting on Declan's

lap? Why is there a guy who looks like he should be changing my tires shining some evil light in my eyes?

I struggle in Declan's arms as I try to figure out what's going on.

"Jade, do you need to throw up again?" Claire asks, pushing a dishpan toward me.

I fight to sit up straight as I mumble, "No, I don't think so."

The guy in blue coveralls directs, "Ma'am, stay still." He turns to Declan and asks as he shines a flashlight in my face, "So, she didn't hit her head?"

The additional light is enough to make me cry out and want to gag again.

"Is that really necessary? Have you ever heard of light sensitivity? She has a freakin' migraine!" Declan hisses.

"I have to ascertain she doesn't have a head injury, sir," Coverall Guy replies. "I wish you'd let me put her on a backboard."

Another person comes to the room and I realize Coverall Guy must be a paramedic because this guy is pushing a gurney thing. Coverall Guy's words finally sink in. "Backboard? Why would I need a backboard? I have a stupid headache like I always get." I look down at the disgusting wet blotches on my clothes and begrudgingly admit, "The only difference this time is I guess I threw up all over myself. I rarely do that. I must be overtired or something."

An unreadable expression crosses Declan's face as he quietly corrects me in a sad, somber tone, "No, J. You passed out. Right in the middle of dessert. I couldn't even wake you up — that's why I called the paramedics."

"I'm sorry for all the drama, but I'm sure it's just a stupid headache. I'll be fine after I take my migraine medicine and get a little rest," I insist.

"Ma'am, I think we need to take you in. It's unusual for someone your age to get such severe migraines without a reason," the paramedic driving the gurney instructs.

Connor walks over to where Declan and I are sitting. He looks down at me and shakes his head as he states, "I want you to listen to me close, Missy; my missus and my son are close to you and my other son is alive because of you. I won't have you be as dumb as me and put off taking care yourself. My own stupidity almost cost me my life. I don't want to see you make the same mistakes. Please, for me, go to the doctor and have yourself checked out. It would give me and the missus some peace of mind."

I glance up at Declan's tense face. "Will you be there with me?"

Declan nods. "Of course. Every step of the way."

As they fasten the last strap on the gurney, I call out to Claire, "Claire, I'm sorry I ruined your whole dinner."

Claire laughs out loud. "I see how my son holds on to you as if his life depends on it. I have a feeling we'll have many, many more family dinners to attend together."

Chapter Eighteen

Declan

IT'S INCREDIBLY DIFFICULT TO watch them poke and prod at Jade when I know she's in so much pain. Usually, her personality fills the room, but she's so out of it right now she looks positively tiny against the stark white sheets of the hospital bed.

At least we're in a private room now where it's not as noisy; when we first came in, we were in a large room with several beds. There were victims of car accidents all around us and one person with food poisoning, who was complaining quite loudly about her predicament. The astonishing cacophony of sound was giving *me* a headache. Eventually after doing preliminary blood work and an MRI, which caused Jade to cry out despite her best efforts to remain stoic, they moved us here. Eventually, Jade gave into the pain medication and went to sleep.

As I watch her doze fitfully, I try to tamp down my panic. I don't see the calm efficiency which surrounded my dad's care. It makes me wonder what's actually going on with her. Although many of the doctors and nurses seem to be dismissive and skeptical about her level of pain - as if she would make all of this up - another contingent of them seem to be very concerned about something. Although, they are not saying anything out loud at this point. They keep adding more and more tests and asking me additional questions about Jade's family history.

I have gotten to know Jade better than anyone I've ever known over the past few months and by extension I've grown closer to Jett and Diamond, but I don't know them nearly well enough to give any of Jade's medical history. The only thing I know is Onyx must've had some medical issues. I don't know the answers and something tells me the doctors think they might hold the key.

I'm confused about whether I should be treating this like a routine event or a matter of life and death, and the hospital personnel isn't giving me any clear guidance. I can't seem to tame the thoughts in my head as I replay the moment she lost consciousness at dinner over and over. I thought my heart would stop on the spot. My dad grew pasty pale and his breathing sped up, but apparently the pacemaker did its job. My mom is fit to be tied. She would like to be here with me at the hospital, but she needs to stay home with my dad since he recently got out of the cardiac rehab unit. Finn drove me here but went back home to be with Mom and Dad.

While Jade is sleeping, I am alone with my thoughts. Put simply, my thoughts are a scary place right now. First, I almost lost my brother, and it looks very much like I could have lost Jade. I don't know if that's true or not but at the moment my heart doesn't really care. All I can think about is what my life would look like without her in it and it's not a pretty sight. I want to be arguing with Jade about whether we should mow the lawn in a checkerboard pattern or diagonally. I know it sounds stupid but I love what our life together has become.

If you had told me all those months ago that I would want to put down roots and shop for garage door openers and mailbox locks, I would've told you that you were absolutely crazy. There is something about being in love with Jade which allows me to find freedom within myself instead of having to look for it everywhere else. It's the weirdest thing. The insatiable drive to conquer my wanderlust is gone. I have found the one place in the world I want to be. I want to be by Jade's side forever. Given my past, that's a big statement to make, but it's where I'm at.

Jade mumbles my name in her sleep. I rush over to her side and grab her hand. "I'm here. What do you need?"

"Hospital sucks," she declares sleepily as she grimaces in pain.

"I agree. I think we've had this conversation once or twice."

"I stink, smell like puke," she complains.

I shrug as I respond, "I'll agree, it's not my favorite perfume on you but it's not the worst thing which could've happened to you today." I walk over to the hospital sink and run hot water. "Wouldn't be the first time I've cleaned up puke in my life. Looks like they've got baby soap here or pink stuff, which would you prefer?"

"Declan, are we supposed to start doing stuff? Don't we have to ask permission?"

"We're hospital experts by now, remember? If we don't bother your IV, I don't think they care much. Besides, didn't you do the same thing for me when I was in the hospital? I vaguely remember being totally covered in blood and you washing me," I tease, hoping to draw a smile and lighten the mood.

"Yeah, but that was different. You were having a hygiene emergency. If the blood and grime had dried on you, you would have been an itchy mess. You were not in any position to scratch yourself back then."

"Oh well, then I declare this a hygiene emergency. You'll be very uncomfortable if you stay sticky and dirty. In order to preserve your mental health, I'm going to clean you up."

Jade gives me a weak grin. "Wow, you're good at this. I think I would like the baby soap please. The other kind smells funky. Funk on top of funk is never good."

I don't see a dishpan around anywhere so I have to ring out the washcloth and carry it over. I do my best to carefully wash every inch of Jade I can reach. I stop briefly when I see the tiny butterfly with the angel wings and the body composed from a semicolon. I've seen this tattoo on her neckline behind her ear hundreds of times; I thought I understood the meaning of it. It wasn't until the incident with Rowan that I truly understood what it meant to pause and take a breath. I will never look at a semicolon the same way.

"You know Jade, I never got a chance to say thank you. Not everyone would have been as brave or patient as you were the other night. Because of you, things will be okay with Rowan."

"I can't take all the credit," Jade responds with a self-deprecating shrug. "Rowan was in a tough spot. He'll be stronger soon."

Around the time I've moved down to Jade's feet, the ER doctor comes in holding a clipboard. When she notices what I'm doing, she smiles at Jade, "Wow, aren't you a lucky one. I wish I'd been able to convince my husband to do that for me when I was pregnant. My feet kind of disappeared."

Jade nods. "I've hit the boyfriend lottery for sure."

The doctor consults her clipboard. "There are still a couple of tests I'm waiting for, but I'd like to see you stay here for a while. Your migraines are atypical and some of your tests are concerning."

Jade struggles to sit up in bed and becomes alarmingly pale. After I crank up the head of her bed, she addresses the doctor. "I don't really need to stay in the hospital for a headache, do I? I've had these headaches for as long as I can remember. I need to sleep it off in a dark room with something cold on my head. I don't sleep well at the hospital. I tried to do it when my grandparents had to spend time in the rehab center after their strokes, but it didn't work very well."

"I can't make you stay, but I think your migraines are more than run-of-the-mill headaches. The episode you had today was serious and we need to find out what caused it," the doctor reasons.

"I don't know; it seems like a lot for headaches I've had forever."

"Could you deal with the pain level you've got right now at home?" the doctor asks Jade with a raised eyebrow.

Jade slumps in the bed "Probably not for long."

"Then we need to keep you here until we figure out what's going on."

Jade looks so defeated. I feel terrible for even calling the ambulance.

"Thank you, we'll talk about it and let you know what we decide," I say, as I shake her hand.

The doctor looks back at Jade. "Ms. Petros, if you care to be honest with the nurse about your pain level, I'll order more pain medicine so you can take a full breath and open your eyes without wincing."

"Jade, I think you should listen to the doctor," I plead. "It's not normal to be in as much pain as you are. Let them take care of you."

Jade glares at me — or at least she tries to — as she huffs, "I thought you were supposed to be on my side."

"Always, J. Even when it's hard for you to tell," I whisper softly.

As I wait for Jett to pick up the phone, I know the move I've made will make me about as popular as bug spray at a mosquito convention, but deep down, I know it's the right thing to do. I hope at some point in our lives, Jade forgives me.

"Go for Jett," he greets brusquely.

"H-hello sir, this is Declan, I'm sorry to disturb your night," I stumble over my words.

"You planning to bring her home anytime soon or is she growing roots in Jax?" he demands.

"Well… um… that's why I'm calling," I stammer. "I'd like to see her delay coming home a bit. I think she's worried about letting everyone down, but she really needs to stay here."

"What are you saying? Stop pussyfooting around. What's going on?"

"Jade had a really bad migraine today. I had to call the ambulance because I couldn't get her to wake up. She is here at the hospital having a few tests and the doctor said they would like to admit her."

"Well, then she should be admitted," Jett asserts, his voice getting louder with every word. "What's the big deal? She has insurance. Have them do whatever they need to do to make her better. She's had those headaches for years. I thought she was getting them treated. She takes medicine for them."

"Jett, I don't know. I've seen her with several migraines, but this one was worse than any I've ever seen before. Honestly, it was almost as scary as my dad's heart attack. I thought she might die right in front of me.

You know Jade — she doesn't want to stay at the hospital. She thinks it's one of her normal, average, everyday headaches she can treat with Excedrin. All you have to do is take one good look at her to know that it's not true. Unfortunately, she's not seeing the risk. She wants to go home and be comfortable. I suspect the doctors think it's something more serious this time but I don't know for sure. I think it's important for you guys to be here. I hope I'm not freaking you guys out over nothing, but something in my gut tells me she might need you to get through this," I ramble on until I run out of steam.

When I'm greeted with absolute silence on the other end of the phone, I wonder if I've made an egregious error.

Finally, Jett lets out a growl of frustration as he admits, "I love that little independent icicle of mine, but she drives me crazy. Sometimes I want to shake her and tell her it's okay to ask for help."

"I'm hoping it turns out to be nothing. The more realistic part of me suspects the easy stuff would've been fixed by now. I think we're on to the tough stuff."

"For once, I hope you're wrong. Take good care of my baby."

"I will. I can't imagine my life without her," I respond as I hang up the phone.

CHAPTER NINETEEN

JADE

OKAY. FINE. I'M HERE. Everybody is freaking thrilled. Everybody except *me*. I personally think the administrators who build and run hospitals should have to sleep in the rooms. Seriously? Who sound proofs these things? Did I *really* need to know Mr. Smith's catheter in Room 523 keeps coming out because he has a fondness for the Playboy Channel on his iPad? No. I did *not*. Nor did I need to memorize the walking pattern of every nurse and other miscellaneous employee on this floor; but since everybody's shoes squeak and the closed door blocks out absolutely nothing, I don't have much choice.

I love Declan, I really do. Even so, sometimes he drives me nuts. Yesterday was a perfect example. I tried to reason with him about why I needed to go home. He was so stubborn — he never stopped insisting he loved me so much he wanted to keep me in the safest environment possible. I swear he recruited half the staff of the hospital to help persuade me to stay. Finally, I gave up. It frustrates me that he doesn't understand I've been dealing with these stupid migraines ever since I can remember. I've tried a bunch of stuff but so far nothing seems to help much.

When I was on the television show and we were filming in Los Angeles, they even sent someone out to fix the feng shui in my bedroom and someone else to align my chakras. I've had all sorts of piercings and acupuncture and tried just about every medication under the sun. None of it's been more effective than a couple of anti-inflammatory pills and ice on the back of my neck. Although, my headaches do seem much worse recently. I don't know if it's because of all the reminders of Onyx, the stress with Dad about Ink'd Deep or because I'm not as young as I once was, but the migraines are wearing on me. What used to be a sometimes-thing is starting to be an almost-always thing. I guess if I'm truly honest with myself, maybe Declan is right. Maybe I need to stay here and figure out what the heck is wrong with me. Still, it's so frustrating.

I'm startled out of my morose thoughts by a knock on the door. I expect it to be Declan, but I am surprised when I see Finn hesitantly standing in the doorway. He's holding a brightly colored gift bag.

"Don't just stand there if you've got presents!" I tease. "There has to be an upside to this place somewhere."

Finn walks up to the edge of the bed and says, "For the record, I only got this because Middle Brother A said you would enjoy it. I'm still a little peeved at you."

Of all the things I was expecting Finn to feel, mad was not it. "Peeved at me? What did I do to you?"

"Because of you I will have more gray hairs than I can count. You about gave me a heart attack. Why didn't you let us know you weren't feeling well at dinner? We could've helped you sooner. I swear, Jade, you looked like you died right there on the spot. You were so pale you seemed like one of those shapeshifter characters on TV."

I'm used to the slightly cynical side of Finn. It is disconcerting to see him shaken up and concerned over my well-being.

"I'm sorry Finn. I'm so used to the migraines that I try to ignore them most of the time. I figured I would wait until after your mom's dinner was over before I went to lie down. I didn't anticipate all this drama. I certainly didn't expect to end up here."

Finn nods as he concedes, "Makes sense." He smiles as he hands me the bag. "I understand you might get a kick out of this."

I open the bag and find a large iPad with a drawing pen. I glance back up at him in shock as I ask, "You're giving me an iPad with a stylus? One of the humungous ones? I know how much those cost. I priced them out for the shop to do tattoo consultations. That's way too much for a present. I mean, maybe I could see it if I had donated a kidney or something, but I just have a headache," I protest.

Finn chuckles and smirks at me as he says, "Yeah, there is definitely no doubt. You *are* much different from Shannon. She would've gobbled that thing up and asked for one in a different color."

"Tell me you're kidding. Don't people have any self-respect anymore?" I ask rhetorically.

Finn shakes his head and mutters, "Not so much and I have the battle scars to prove it." He speaks louder as he points to the iPad. "Don't worry about that. Not long ago, I helped an executive at Apple find an antique car he was looking for at a bargain price. He handed those out like they were playing cards."

"You should totally give one to Declan, he uses them to compose his music since he hurt his hand. I think he would find the large one even more helpful than mine," I suggest, thinking how much easier it would be for Declan to play the piano on the bigger screen.

Finn shakes his head in bemusement. "I've already taken care of Middle Brother A. Declan tried to tell me you were this nice, but I didn't really believe him. You're making a believer out of me. Maybe unicorns do exist —"

I'm trying to follow this conversation, I am — but I'm so confused. Of course, it could have something to do with the fact that I got like, no sleep last night, but unicorns? "What are you talking about — did you skip your morning coffee?"

Finn chuckles softly. "Never mind, I guess you had to be there. I'll leave this here with you because I need to get to work. I hope they can figure out what's hurting you."

He pats my foot on the way out the door and I'm left to puzzle over his unexpected generosity.

I wake up to the sound of pages turning in a book. This is not unusual — Declan reads a lot. Trust me, when I have a migraine, the sound of rustling paper is like jet engines. It's discouraging to me that even though I'm in the hospital with all sorts of medications at the doctors' disposal, they still haven't been able to knock down my migraines to a manageable level. I look over to the recliner chair expecting to find Declan enthralled in his latest novel. He's on a crime thriller binge reading kick these days.

Much to my shock, I see my mom engrossed in a book. When I let out a surprised gasp, a voice from the other side of the room emerges. "Mornin', Jade. Feeling any better?" inquires my dad.

I shrug. "You know, kind of the usual. What are you doing here?"

"Baby, you're in the hospital. Where would you expect us to be?" my mom counters with a confused expression on her face

"If it weren't for my meddling boyfriend, you probably wouldn't know about my little field trip here until after it was all over and I wouldn't have to worry you guys half to death."

"I'm grateful the young man had the good sense to call us. We needed to be here for you. Sometimes I wish you weren't so hardheaded like me." My dad kisses me on the cheek.

From the shadows, Declan steps forward and hands me a cup from a nearby coffee place and a delicious looking pastry. "I figured you might want a break from the hospital food, so I brought you a treat — chai tea with extra cinnamon. Has the doctor been in yet this morning?"

"No, they did a bunch of tests last night after I made you go home and get some rest, so he might be waiting for results. All I know is the technician was making all sorts of frowny-faces while she was doing the exam. It made my skin crawl."

The neurologist pokes his head around the door and remarks, "I swear I felt my ears burning? Were you all talking about me?"

Not willing to miss a chance to deliver a barb, my dad retorts, "Yeah, we were. We were wondering if you had enough time between your golf games to come in and talk to my daughter."

"Although I do like a good golf game, this particular morning, I was helping to repair a brain aneurysm, but thanks for asking," the neurologist responds.

I cringe. "I apologize for my dad. Sometimes, he thinks he's funny."

The doctor looks at me and grins. "I think that's a common ailment, so I don't take offense." His expression grows somber as he pulls up a round spinning chair next to my bed and sits down. He spreads out a bunch of ominous looking pictures on my bed. "Unfortunately, we have to talk about some serious stuff."

"How serious?" Declan comes around the other side of the bed to hold my hand.

"It's one of those good news and bad news situations," the neurologist explains. "The good news is I think I found a definitive cause of your migraines and why they don't respond well to medications."

"What's the bad news?" I ask in a voice so small, I hardly recognize it as my own.

The neurologist pulls out a black-and-white picture with splashes of blue and red. As he points to the picture with his pen, he says, "What you're looking at here is a sizable PFO in your heart; it means that blood is going directly from one chamber to the other in a direction it's not supposed to be traveling. This has been associated with an increase in migraines and stroke. I understand your family has a substantial history of stroke as well."

"Oh … No … It's true. She has it on both sides of

the family," my mom confirms under her breath.

"Wait — you're saying Jade has an extra hole in her heart?" Declan asks after studying the pictures closely.

"That's exactly what I'm saying. We all start out that way when the heart forms, but usually it seals up in utero before we're born. For whatever reason, Jade's did not. It's a common deficit. A lot of people don't even have any symptoms. However, Jade's hole is large and she is having debilitating problems. With her family history of strokes, she should get the hole surgically repaired."

"My dad had open heart surgery. It was brutal. Are you sure that's the best approach?" Declan probes.

"Fortunately, we can repair it through a catheter in her leg and it won't require opening her chest," he explains to Declan.

I'm still trying to sort out all the words which were dumped in my lap. Somehow I'm supposed to make sense of migraine, heart, hole and surgery all in one sentence. "Let me get this straight: I came into the hospital with a headache and now I have to have heart surgery to make it better?" I ask. "On what planet does that even make any sense?"

"Mother Nature is a fickle thing, these things rarely ever make sense. We fix them the best we can."

"What happens if I do nothing?" I ask, thinking of all the medical horror stories I've seen in the news recently.

"Like I said, for most folks it's not a big deal. Because of your headaches and history of strokes, I think it's a bigger issue. I would strongly recommend you pursue it. I want you to arrange a follow-up visit with a cardiac specialist and I'll be happy to forward all your testing to whoever you would like to see for a second opinion. This is too important to be sloppy about," the doctor advises.

"Do you think this will help her headaches?" Declan asks.

"I can't make any guarantees. The literature is mixed but a lot of patients report a huge improvement."

"Jade, did you hear him? A huge improvement. That would make a major difference in your life," Declan offers, sounding encouraged.

"I know, but I'm still stuck on the words 'heart surgery'. I never guessed that at my age, I would be facing heart surgery."

The neurologist smiles. "Every patient I talk to regardless of age says about the same thing. I know it's a big decision, but I think in your case it would be warranted."

"When can I go home?" I ask, feeling a little petulant and obstinate.

"I'll try to coordinate it with whoever's in charge of the floor today, but we should be able to get you out of here by this afternoon. I'll make referrals to some specialists so we can see what we can do to reduce your headaches. I'm sorry it has to be so dramatic."

After the doctor leaves the room, I flop against the pillows and exclaim, "A hole in my heart? Can you even believe that?"

My mom draws in a shaky breath and lets out a little sob.

As he walks over to her and pulls her up into an embrace, my dad asks, "You okay?"

My mom nods against his neck and shudders. She

pulls away and explains, "All this is scary, but I'm thinking back to when Onyx was little. Do you remember this, Jett? Onyx used to go around with a little medical set and pretend to be a doctor. He used to listen to your chest, Jade. He would come to me with a sad expression on his face and announce there was something wrong with your heart. I always dismissed him because I figured he was pretending. Now I wonder if your brother knew something all those years ago. He was always crazy overprotective of you."

My eyes tear up. "Onyx was always exceptionally perceptive. It wouldn't surprise me if he knew all along."

I'm shocked my dad allowed Declan to drive me home from the hospital. I'm well aware of the fact that I'm an adult — but sometimes my dad forgets. If there was ever an excuse for him to forget, learning I need heart surgery is probably one of them. I'm still having a hard time with the concept myself.

When Declan returns to our picnic table with jerk chicken and grilled vegetables from this amazing food truck we found, I can't keep it together anymore. I'll miss being able to do all of these things together. I don't see how we can manage this. Declan has enough going on in his life between his dad and his brother, he doesn't need one more thing with me.

I feel like I'm being torn in a million different directions. Part of me doesn't want to do the surgery at all. It seems risky for mere headaches — but then I remember taking care of my grandparents after their strokes. Strokes are nothing to mess with.

Understandably, my parents want me back in Gainesville so they can take care of me. Honestly, I want to be wherever Declan is. Sadly, the logistics of that are a nightmare and whenever I think about it, my emotions get the best of me.

After Declan arranges the food in front of me, he looks up and catches my expression. Immediately he rushes around the table. He scoots me forward on the wooden plank and sits behind me and envelops me in a full body hug. "Talk to me, J," he whispers against my hair.

"I'm scared," I admit, as I lean back against his chest. "How will we survive this?"

"With grace, humor and together," Declan declares as he kisses the top of my head.

I take a deep breath as I decide those words will become my personal mantra for whatever is coming.

Chapter Twenty

Declan

I REMEMBER AS A kid I always wanted my life to be very exciting. Right now, I could live with a little less excitement. Okay, if I'm honest I could live with a *lot* less excitement. I had no idea when I first asked Jade to go out to lunch on that crazy, chaotic day, everything in my life would change so dramatically. Granted, she's not the cause of all of it, but it's all tangled together like a demented kite string. It's like my life could be like one of those beautiful, artistic kites which fly in the festivals every year — if I could only keep it balanced. Right now, it's as if I've made no progress from the defeated seven-year-old I was when I first tried to learn to fly a kite. I feel like I'm dragging my life behind me through the sand and hoping it survives.

It's a good thing my dad sells cars because I spend an ungodly amount of time on the road between Jacksonville and Gainesville. It's a crazy commute — but it's not as crazy as Jade's friend, Tristan. He offered to provide a helicopter for me to use. When he offered, I had to look around to make sure it wasn't some big elaborate joke, but I'll be darned if he wasn't serious.

The other crazy thing is my dad is paying for me to

work for Stone Auto Group. With all the time I spend in Gainesville to be with Jade, I don't know how he justifies it. I make a few sales here and there, but nothing like Finn and Rowan. Frankly, I'm too distracted. If I'm at work, I'm thinking about Jade and if I'm with Jade, I'm thinking about Dad and Rowan. I feel like a hamster who can't get off the exercise wheel.

As I pull my car into the driveway, I notice my dad is working on his favorite vintage car. As I get out of my car, he advises, "Time to get those brakes looked at, they squeak."

It's not a huge request, and he's absolutely right — but today it's too much. I lean back against my car and scrub my hand down my face as I fight back tears.

"You all right, son?" My dad searches my face for clues.

I start to reflexively answer in the socially acceptable, polite manner we all automatically do, but I stop and decide I can't do this anymore. "Actually, no. I'm not all right. I need to be everywhere at once and I can't be. I feel like I'm letting everyone down and helping no one."

My dad pulls a lawn chair over and motions for me to sit down.

"My girlfriend has a hole in her heart, Dad — it's a *freakin' hole.* I had to listen to another specialist today tell us if we do something, there's a risk she dies. If we don't do something, there's a bigger risk she dies of something different. How do you choose between two horrible maybes? How do you choose when the doctors don't agree? There was this one article I read online which said this PFO surgery might not even fix her migraines. On top of that, even if we decide to do the surgery, there are different methods to do it and they don't agree on how to do it even. Some doctors use shunts, other doctors use patches and other doctors stitch it up. It's like you need a medical degree to figure out what they're even talking about or how to choose the best doctor to go with," I confess, unloading all of my day on my dad's shoulders.

"I know what you're talking about, we ran into that with the options for the bypass rehab. Everybody has a slightly different philosophy. I don't know how they expect patients to choose," my dad commiserates.

"Dad, I don't know how I can continue to be here for you and Rowan and give enough focus to Jade. I'm so exhausted. It is a good thing I have the roads memorized between here and Gainesville. If I had to think about it too hard, my brain would probably explode."

"So stop," my dad answers succinctly.

"Stop what?" I ask, embarrassed that I must've lost track of the conversation.

"Stop trying to be everything for everyone," my dad clarifies. "When I first asked you to step in at Stone Auto, the doctors told me I shouldn't be working. In case you missed it, I'm fully cleared to work now. In fact, I've been putting in more hours than any of my sons combined. Your excuse for hanging around here to fill in for me is gone."

"But what about Rowan? He's made some progress with his therapy and his medication. If I suddenly yank myself out of the situation, won't it make things worse?"

"Declan, you weren't responsible for Rowan's problem, you won't be responsible for the fix. His doctor told us it was some sort of imbalance in his brain chemistry and he's doing much better on the medication.

He is seeing a headshrinker to help him with all the crap Shannon put him through. They've got a safety plan in place now and we are all more aware. I think he'll be fine, but even if he's not, you've got someone else you need to take care of."

"Dad, what if something happens to Jade? I just figured it all out with her. She's what makes my life make sense. If she's not all right, I don't know what I'll do," I blurt.

"Son, you have to think positive. You've got to plan for what happens if everything works out exactly the way it is supposed to."

My dad's words echo in my brain as I pull up to the beer pub that's a few blocks from Jade's place. This is an admittedly scary step on the way to having things work out the way they're supposed to. My relationship with Jett is hard to figure out. Although there are times when I think he truly respects me, there are other times he seems to look at me like I'm the twelve-year-old kid who broke his picture window with a baseball. I wonder which Jett I'll encounter today.

"You want to tell me what we're doing here at four-thirty on a Thursday afternoon? My afternoon is slammed," Jett greets me gruffly as he pulls out a chair, turns it around and sits down on it backwards.

"Do you want the practical answer or the theoretical answer?" I quip, handing him a bucket of pretzels.

One eyebrow wings up as he crosses his arms and answers, "Surprise me."

I take a deep breath and plunge forward as I respond,

"Okay, the practical reason is Jade can't eat anything but liquids tonight and I don't want to eat in front of her."

"That's big of you, considering the fact my only daughter is having heart surgery tomorrow. It's a risky thing."

"Trust me sir, I have not forgotten. I've thought of little else since the diagnosis. It's the first thing I consider when I wake up and it's my last thought when I go to sleep. The possibility of losing your daughter terrifies me. I love her more than I can ever express in words."

"That's a mighty big statement for a guy who makes his living with words."

my beer and pop a pretzel in my mouth. After a few moments, I summon the courage to be brutally honest. "As a songwriter, I thought I had a good handle on what it means to be in love. Since I met Jade, I've discovered I knew absolutely nothing about love. Jade has shown me you don't have to change who you are to impress the person who truly loves you — you simply have to be the best you can be."

Jett blinks slowly and then warns, "You know, it's not all rainbows and butterflies. Real love hurts. It hurts in ways you never expect."

"I'm prepared for that. Whatever we face, we are stronger together," I answer nervously. "Umm... I'm going to stop beating around the bush and just ask. Jett Petros, I love your daughter very much and I'm respectfully asking your permission to marry her."

A slow grin passes over Jett's face. "What do you know? I owe my lovely wife a dinner out because she bet me this would be the topic of today's little get together. I'm not sure how she knew, but she pretty much knows everything."

"Does she know if you'll say yes?" I ask cautiously.

"What do you think? My wife and daughter both believe the sun and moon rise and fall at your feet. If I told you no, there would be hell to pay. But, mark my words. You put another hole in my daughter's heart and I'll put multiple holes in you."

"Understood. To be clear … that's a yes, right?" I stammer.

"I can't believe I'm saying this, but yes, you have my blessing. I think I need to go to the doctor. I just gave permission for my only daughter to marry a largely unemployed musician."

"I'll do my best to make sure you don't regret your decision, sir," I promise.

CHAPTER TWENTY-ONE

JADE

I SUCK AT PRETENDING. There's no two ways about it. I feel bad too because everyone is working diligently to act like today isn't a big deal and it's something like going to the mall. I've been over this decision a million times in my head and Declan and I have done so much research we could probably become lecturers on the subject. In the moments I'm being absolutely candid with myself, I honestly don't know with one hundred percent certainty surgery is the best answer. On the other hand, I don't know it's not the best answer either. Declan and I factored in my family history and stuck our thumb on the scales toward doing the surgery. I hope to God I am making the right decision.

"Jade, why does your phone keep going off every thirty seconds?" Marcus asks as he pauses his elaborate story to glare at my phone.

"Apparently, somebody stole the batteries out of both Mom and Dad's cars overnight and he has to wait for the auto shop to bring him another one. He is fit to be tied because he's afraid they'll miss my surgery. I told him not to worry about it, but he's having a conniption fit anyway."

"Oh man, that bites. Did he have his security system on?" asks Tristan.

"I don't know. You're the one who put it in for him, did you make it Dad-proof?" I joke.

"If Identity Bank did it, your dad will never be able to accidentally turn it off, I've seen Tristan's crew at work. They wired a security system into a house where I was house-sitting. It was like Fort Knox and the Pentagon all wrapped up into one," Declan comments.

Ivy smirks, "Marcus, remember when we went to a party at Tristan's house and we got a little hot and heavy in the closet?"

Marcus blushes. "Yeah, I'm not likely to forget anytime soon. His security detail still looks at us funny when we get on the plane. Seriously? Who puts a full color twenty-mega-pixel security camera in a closet? I still maintain it wasn't our fault if they got an eyeful."

Rogue laughs as she places her arm around Tristan's waist. "You guys remember the good old days when this guy was shy? Yeah, not so much anymore. Between us and our parents, they've seen more than they should have in their jobs."

"I think it's cute your parents are still like frisky newlyweds after all these years," I interject.

"I know I'm a little late to the party," Declan comments, "but aren't they technically still newlyweds?"

"I guess it depends on how you count their years of marriage," Ivy responds. "Rogue and I like to believe Mama Rosa and Padre-Pop were never actually 'unmarried' because their marriage vows had no beginning or end. Life circumstances just got in the way."

"On the other hand, if they want to play up the

newlywed aspect of their marriage, more power to them—"

Inexplicably, Declan gets up and paces around the room. He compulsively checks the door. I know he's probably as nervous about the surgery as I am, but he's been relatively calm this morning; in fact, he's been my anchor during all this craziness. He's been the voice of reason and logic. He's also been the voice of hopefulness and faith. He sees no reason this won't go exactly as planned, so he doesn't even seem worried ... much. This behavior is odd; it's like a light switch has been flipped in him.

I was thinking there weren't beds in the hospital more uncomfortable than the ones I stayed in when I was here the last time, but I guess I've never been in the surgery prep beds. This thing is as hard as a rock. A nurse came in before to put in my IV but she was called away. We've been waiting here for what seems like forever.

Finally, my dad peeks his head in the room. "I guess this is the right place," he comments, as he looks around and sees all of my friends.

Under his breath, Declan murmurs something to my dad. I can't catch it all but it has something to do with leaving him enough time.

I look over to my mom for clues, but she shrugs.

Suddenly, Declan addresses everyone in the room when he says, "I'm glad you are all here to support Jade, you are some of the most important people in her life. It's only appropriate that you're here on this day."

I am completely exhausted because I haven't slept worth beans for several weeks. For the life of me, I cannot figure out why Declan is suddenly talking like a narrator at a movie. I mean it's not like he doesn't see these people almost every day. I meet Rogue's gaze across the room and she shrugs too.

By the time I look for Declan again, he's kneeling — wait… he's *kneeling*! No way! This is what happens to all my friends. This doesn't happen to me and it especially doesn't happen on the scariest day of my whole life. He is so *not* doing this. He *better* not be doing this. I'm not dressed up, I have no makeup on — in fact they told me not to wear makeup. My hair is in some crazy paper hairnet and I've got blue booties on my feet.

I peek through my fingers to see if I've seen what I thought I saw. I did. There he is, the love of my life kneeling on the floor of a hospital holding out a beautiful ring box. I hold my breath and wait as he says, "Jade, we are bound to face a lot of scary times together. This may be one of the scariest, and I can't let you go into surgery without knowing whether you'll marry me. I first fell in love with the person I thought you would be. Honestly, it was an unrequited crush from afar, you seemed to be every guy's perfect dream, but the real you turned out to be so much better than I ever imagined you would be. I love that you don't want to get out of bed on the weekends until you've completed every word game in the newspaper, including the crossword puzzles. I love that you know every Jackson Browne song ever done but when we go dancing you know more stuff that's being played on the radio than most of the DJs. I love that you see life in pictures and colors, phrases and poems. I love that when you look at me you see the real me — the person I am at my core and you respect me for just being me. You never tried to change who I am to suit you. For those reasons and so many more, Jade Crystal Petros, will you agree to be my wife so our love story continues into infinity?"

I have to catch my breath as his words wash over me. For a brief second, I consider the possibility things may not go well and I might become some vegetable he would have to take care of his whole life if I make this commitment. It only takes one look at the open, loving expression on his face to tell me that even if the worst were to happen, he would be by my side until the end.

I take a deep breath as I pull my hand out from under the covers and extend it for him to place the ring on. I feel cold metal slide over my ring finger and settle into place. It's heavier than I expected and when I pull my hand back, it's all I can do not to shriek with delight. The ring is perfect. It's a series of Celtic knots woven into a solid band. It is perfectly atypical for me and it honors Declan's heritage. I can't think of anything more suited for the two of us.

When I look up to thank Declan for such a perfect ring, I see an expectant look on his face. *Nope, this definitely isn't going the way I scripted it in my head for years and years.*

I flush red hot before I gather the verbal wherewithal to answer his question, "Declan Ailín, I have done enough Celtic knot tattoos to know the type of commitment you're asking from me. When this happened to all of my friends, I watched with amused amazement — and a little green-eyed jealousy as they each found their perfect match. I was convinced it would never happen for me because I was too guarded, complicated and layered with pain. I was certain I would be alone and lonely forever. But, you came along and found a way past all of my walls and gave me the strength to climb over them, through them, and around them to be the real me. I love you Declan and I will be honored to wear this ring forever. Yes, I will marry you."

I am so focused on memorizing the expressions on Declan's face, I fail to notice a small gaggle of nurses has formed in the doorway to my room. After Declan leans down to give me a not-so-PG kiss to celebrate our engagement, wild applause and cheers erupt. A confused looking guy in Daffy Duck scrubs wanders through the chaos with a red tray filled with needles and tubes. "I'm not sure I want to know what happened here, but I have orders from upstairs. The other surgery went faster than they expected so they want us to package you and get you ready to go. I've got to get your IV in and another set of vitals before I can take you up there."

I am a little stunned by the quick change in mood and intensity.

This is it.

Declan takes my hand and slides off my ring. It hardly seems fair, I only got to wear it for a few minutes. Declan sees the tears leaking out of the corners of my eyes and my panic grow. He gently kisses me one more time. "Don't worry, I'll give it back. Infinity is a very long time."

EPILOGUE

DECLAN

IT'S REALLY HARD FOR me to tiptoe through the house when what I want to be doing is triumphantly dancing and declaring victory; but it will have to wait. You see, my fiancée — can I tell you how much I love to use that word? My beautiful fiancée has had far too much time on her hands since the doctors told her not to exert herself for a few weeks. Jade is clearly a master at online ordering and she has been using the iPad Finn gave her to gain the upper hand in the toilet paper wars. Her latest entries were pure genius. She got me Sudoku puzzles. Practical and funny. Her next one was funnier still after she caught me trying to solve the Sudoku puzzles one night. A couple days later, the new roll of toilet paper appeared on my designated dispenser. This new toilet paper looked exactly like parking tickets. I figured this expert level of humor would be hard to top, so I've decided to go for sentimental and I bought some which says, "I love you from top to bottom." It even has little red roses.

I can hardly contain my anticipatory glee as I tiptoe past her. She's taking a nap on the couch with Inkblot lying squarely on her shoulder. Although she's been a little tired, the absolute miracle is that she no longer seems to be in constant pain. She got a headache the other day —

it about scared us to death. She was afraid everything would come back, even after all she'd gone through. Fortunately, it turned out to be an average run-of-the-mill headache and she knocked it down with a couple of Motrin.

After I successfully hang my new surprise in the bathroom, I cover Jade with a blanket, scoop Inkblot up into my arms and carry him into the office. Jade gave me my own corner for composing and songwriting. Lately I've been putting it to a slightly different use as well. When I worked with my family at the car lot, I started calling all of my customers after they purchased cars to see how well everything was going. My dad was so impressed by how well this technique works to encourage customers to come back to buy cars for their spouses or their children, he has instituted the program for all of his car sales. In essence, I am telecommuting and still working for Stone Auto Group. My mom is absolutely thrilled because having me involved in the business is taking some of the burden off of my dad's shoulders. It's working surprisingly well for me too. I never thought I could make peace with my family. I always assumed we would be too different to work together. It feels remarkably good to be working toward the same family goal and still be able to write music.

As I flip through my mail, I'm surprised to see a letter from Silent Beats Music. I am so shocked I almost drop it. Immediately, I wonder if it's some sort of scam. Why would Aidan O'Brien's music label contact me? This isn't any corporate music label — it's one he started himself. Rumor has it he handpicks every talent on his label. I open the small brown envelope with a great deal of skepticism and even more hope.

Oddly, all it contains is an oversized post-it-note with a few handwritten lines:

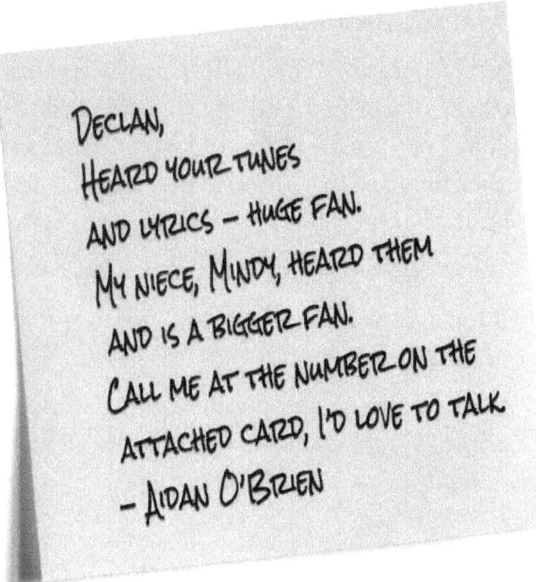

With shaking hands, I put the Post-it note on the desk and pick up the phone to call Joe Summers. In a voice I barely recognize as my own, I ask, "Hey, I heard from Aidan O'Brien — he says he's heard my stuff. Do you know anything about it?"

"Yeah, I got signed by his label a couple months ago. I called the house to tell you, but you were at work, so your girlfriend answered. I asked her if she thought you would mind if I played a few of your demo tapes for Aidan. She told me you would never push hard enough to give yourself that kind of break because you're always taking care of everyone else. I figured that was probably true since you gave me one of the best written songs I've ever heard."

"You give me royalties off that song," I argue.

"Only because I basically force them on you, I've never had to work so hard to give somebody money in my whole life. Usually in this industry people are after you with their hands out. Anyway, I was telling Aidan about all of our co-writes and he's definitely interested."

"Thank you, man. I don't know what to say."

"Don't thank me, thank your girlfriend. She encouraged me to do it."

After I hang up the phone, I think to myself, *I really am marrying a magical unicorn of a woman and my life will never be the same.*

EPILOGUE

JADE

"MARK, I'M SO SORRY I've had to reschedule on you a couple of times. Who knew my stupid headaches would cause such drama?"

"It's okay, everything about our meeting has been atypical. Why should this be any different?"

There is something strangely intense about Mark Littleson. It's not so much his size, Tristan and Declan are bigger. I don't think it's his looks either, although his Native American features are compellingly attractive. I think it's something about the energy he radiates. Somehow, he manages to be both incredibly exciting and peaceful at the same time.

"Still, it's not the way I like to do business," I insist with a grimace.

"Are you feeling better now?" he asks, his voice filled with concern.

I guess that's perhaps the one thing I've had the hardest time getting used to. All of this pity and concern reminds me of the looks I used to get shortly after Onyx passed away. It's very disconcerting to have to rebuild my personal wall every time someone tries to be nice. I know it's probably not a normal response to people being friendly, but it's what I feel I do.

"My migraines are better — although my usual doctor read me the riot act. Apparently having the surgery is not the recommended treatment now. I don't even know how to answer because my headaches do feel better and nothing before the surgery worked," I babble, not sure why I'm telling him all this superfluous background information.

As I'm sizing the large back piece for Mark and transferring the outline to Mark's back so he can check the scale, I notice I'm getting winded much easier than I have in the past.

"Mark, I hate to tell you this but I may have to do this tattoo in more sessions than we'd planned. My endurance is not what it was before I went in for surgery. This dream catcher is very intricate with lots of line work. I want to make sure I'm strong enough to do it right for you. I'm sorry for any inconvenience," I apologize.

"Like I said before, sometimes the timing of life is out of our hands," he offers philosophically.

I smile wryly. "You're preaching to the choir here. My life over the past few months has been a study in the patient approach."

A smile lights up Mark's face as he glances at my ring. "If I were to venture a guess, I would say you are much happier with your new approach, correct?"

I take a moment to study my engagement ring and all it symbolizes. I take a deep breath and try to shake off the stress as I remember I have everything I could ever need in my life right at this very moment.

I return Mark's grin. "Yes, you are absolutely right. Declan has helped me find the happiness in my life I thought I had lost a long time ago."

"Well … there you go, there's something to be said for new approaches," he quips.

I am still working with Mark's stencil when Rogue comes up and taps me on the shoulder. This is highly unusual for Rogue. Unlike Marcus, she leaves me completely undisturbed when I'm tattooing.

I look up at her. "Need something?"

Rogue is chewing on her bottom lip. "You've been doing this a lot longer than I have. Maybe I'm missing something or more precisely, maybe I'm seeing something which isn't there. Anyway, I'd appreciate it if you could come look at Shelby's back for me."

There is something about Rogue's halting delivery which makes the hair on the back of my neck stand up. She has become a confident tattoo artist, there isn't much she can't handle — in many ways she's already better than me.

I lean over Mark's shoulder and ask him, "Do you mind if we take a break? A colleague needs assistance."

He shakes his head. "That's okay, I've got some messages I need to listen to from work. We've got a case in mediation unless the judge pulls the plug."

"I'll be right back," I assure him.

Rogue and I walk over to her station. Shelby is lying face down on her adjustable bench.

"Sorry to keep you waiting, I'd like Jade to take a look at your back if it's all right with you," Rogue explains. "This is Jade, my boss."

"Oh, I wasn't waiting long. I used to spend longer than this in tanning beds. It was nice to have a moment to myself. I've been so busy with graduation I haven't had a chance to even stop and think about things. I've got so much to do before my trip to Louisiana, my head hurts even thinking about it."

"Shelby, do you mind if I look at your back?" I ask.

"I don't have a problem with that. Do whatever you need to do."

"I noticed the area right above where her bra strap would be. That's the most acute, but she's got a few others with inconsistent texture. They don't appear to be painful because I touched them with my stencil pen and she didn't seem to react."

I change out my gloves to another set of neoprene gloves. I run the edge of my thumb over the area Rogue was concerned about. Even through my glove, I can feel the sandpaper texture of Shelby's skin.

I glance over at Rogue and softly state, "I second your call."

"What does that mean?" Shelby asks, alarmed. "It's usually not this hard for me to get a tattoo. Is it because I chose a dream catcher? Is there some sort of religious prohibition against it?"

"No, not that I know of," I answer. "Shelby, there's no easy way to tell you this — based on our experience, we think you should see a doctor about your back. There seems to be something unusual going on."

"What do you mean 'based on your experience'? What happened? I thought you hadn't even started tattooing yet."

I shift uncomfortably on my feet before answering, but even then I hedge, "We see lots of skin every day and we've seen a lot of different stuff. It might be a good idea to play it safe and have it checked out. Hopefully it's nothing."

"Are you saying you can't tattoo the dream catcher on my back?" Shelby repeats, sounding bewildered.

"I think perhaps what she's saying is right now the timing isn't right," Mark interjects.

"You don't even know me. What could you possibly know about my life?" Shelby asks.

"I know nothing — except that you can't change what will be."

Note from the Author

Dear Reader:

Thank you so much for reading *Hearts of Jade*. The story continues in *Love is More Than Skin Deep*.

Shelby Lyons just wanted to get a tattoo.

Why did something so simple complicate her life?

Mark Littleson specializes in complicated.

As a senior law partner and single father of a child with autism, he doesn't need any more worries in his life

Despite Mark's best intentions, he is compelled to help Shelby.

Far from being a complication, Shelby is the piece of the puzzle he and his daughter have been missing.

When Shelby's health is in question, will Mark learn that Love is More Than Skin Deep?

(This story is inspired by the heroic journey of Judy Noble Cloud.)

You'll love this story of triumph inspired by true life events.

Get *Love is More Than Skin Deep* now!

RESOURCES

If you need immediate assistance, call 9-1-1

National Suicide Prevention Lifeline: 1-800-273-TALK (8255)

TEXT 'Help' to 741741

American Foundation for Suicide Prevention: (http://afsp.org) A comprehensive program that includes educational materials for people at risk of suicide, family members and people affected by suicide. They have outreach offices in all fifty states and include legislative reform to improve the health resources for people at risk for suicide. The website is an incredible resource.

Yellow Ribbon Suicide Prevention Program: (http://yellowribbon.org) An organization dedicated to the prevention of suicide through ensuring that information and resources are readily available and easily accessible to everyone.

Migraine Research Foundation: (https://migraineresearchfoundation.org/) This organization raises funds to support research grants to find a cure for migraine headaches. The website also features several helpful tools to help manage migraines including several migraine diaries, ways to choose doctors and links to support groups.

American Headache and Migraine Association: (https://ahma.memberclicks.net) This organization is focused on bringing patients and care providers together through patient empowerment. It focuses on improving patient and care provider communication and information sharing.

ACKNOWLEDGMENTS

As an author, one of the most common questions I'm asked is which book I've written is my favorite. I will tell you straight off, that it is impossible for an author to tell you which book is their favorite. It is like choosing between your children. It is next to impossible. Having said that, I think without question this novel may be one of my most important to date. In many ways, it's one of my more personal novels, even though it doesn't deal directly with a character with a visible disability.

For much of my career, I was a disability advocate. I will always maintain that invisible disabilities are much more challenging than visible disabilities. Mental illness and chronic depression are the most challenging of all because no one recognizes the struggle. Sometimes, no one sees your pain until it's far too late.

Such was the case in my life when I was attending law school. One of my fellow law students took her own life. Very few of us, if any of us, saw her suicide coming. The ripple effects of Valencia's death followed our whole class for years to come. I will never as long as I live, forget her funeral and hearing her parents comment that Valencia had disclosed to them she thought she had no friends. Nothing could have been further from the truth. If she had only found strength to reach out, they would've been dozens of us willing to help. Such as the nature of the struggle — her vision was clouded by depression and mental illness and she was unable to see clearly. It has been nearly twenty years since her death, but I am still shaken by it today. I will forever wonder if there is something more I could have done.

I wrote this book in her memory in hopes that someone, somewhere who is struggling may find the strength to reach out and find help. There is always someone in the world who cares.

To Kathern Watts and Lacie Redding: Thanks for caring so much about me, yet not caring when I email you at three o'clock in the morning with story ideas. Without you guys, I wouldn't be able to make this engine go.

 To Leonard Crawford: I love you more than words can say, but this is my twelfth book. You can stop telling people this is my hobby. I think I'm a bona fide author by now.

About the Author

I have been lucky enough to live my own version of a romance novel. I married the guy who kissed me at summer camp. He told me on the night we met that he was going to marry me and be the father of my children.

Eventually, I stopped giggling when he said it, and we've been married for more than thirty years. We have two children. The oldest is a Doctor of Osteopathy. He is across the United States completing his residency, but when he's done, he is going to come back to Oregon and practice Family Medicine. Our youngest son is now tackling high school and where he is an honor student. He is interested in becoming an EMT.

I write full time now. I have published more than thirty books and have several more underway. I volunteer my time to a variety of causes. I have worked as a Civil Rights Attorney and diversity advocate. I spent several years working for various social service agencies before becoming an attorney.

In my spare time, I love to cook, decorate cakes and of

course, I obsessively, compulsively read.

I would be honored if you would take a few moments out of your busy day to check out my website, MaryCrawfordAuthor.com. While you're there, you can sign up for my newsletter and get a free book. I will be announcing my upcoming books and giving sneak peeks as well as sponsoring giveaways and giving you information about other interesting events.

If you have questions or comments, please E-mail me at Mary@MaryCrawfordAuthor.com or find me on the following social networks:

Facebook: www.facebook.com/authormarycrawford

Website: MaryCrawfordAuthor.com

Twitter: www.twitter.com/MaryCrawfordAut

www.ingramcontent.com/pod-product-compliance
Lightning Source LLC
Chambersburg PA
CBHW050510190726
48284CB00003B/762